BLOOD STRANGERS

Behind Closed Doors: Family Secrets

VICKI HINZE

D0884997

MAGNOLIA LEAF
PRESS

Blood Strangers

Copyright © 2020 by Vicki Hinze

This is a work of fiction. Names, characters, places, and incidents are the product of the author's imagination or used fictitiously, and any resemblance to actual persons, living or dead, business establishments, events or locales is coincidental.

Published by Magnolia Leaf Press, Niceville, Florida
Print Edition ISBN: 9781939016409
Digital Edition AISN: B08BS5X4MQ
First Edition 2020, Printed in the USA
10 9 8 7 6 5 4 3 2 1

BLOOD STRANGERS

FAMILYSECRETS.LIFE

WHEN BLOOD ISN'T THICKER THAN WATER

They say blood is thicker than water.
I guess it is, until it isn't.
There are occasions when at the first sign of trouble,
family will throw you under the bus . . .
and then run over you.
Water then is thicker than the
bloody roadkill remnants left of you.

— FAMILYSECRETS.LIFE

PROLOGUE

Canal Street
New Orleans, Louisiana
Monday, November 23, 10:30 a.m.

A GRUFF OLD man in an expensive suit walked right up to Gabby Blake on the crowded sidewalk. "Helena?" He looked confused, swiped at his gray temple with a blue-veined hand. "No. No, you can't be Helena."

Gabby nearly dropped the grocery sack in her arms. Her heart raced, her body trembled, and her throat went thick. "You knew Helena?"

He squinted and studied her face. "You look just like my sister's husband, Rogan. Just like him, God rest his soul."

The doors opened on a black SUV parked curbside and two rough-looking men spilled out. They rushed up to the old stranger and grabbed him by the arms. "It's time to go," one of them said in a hushed, urgent tone. "Right now."

Both men stared at Gabby. "Sorry," the one on the old man's left told her. "He forgets . . ."

Ordinarily, Gabby would be guarded and suspicious, but

looking into the old man's eyes, seeing that things weren't as they should be was obvious. Dementia, or something like it, she supposed. Bless his heart. "No problem." She nodded at the newcomer who'd spoken to her. Had it not been for an instinctive warning—something in his eyes, in the way they all looked at her that had gooseflesh rising on her arms and shivers shooting up her spine—she would have asked the old man about Helena. Was it possible? After all this time?

It wasn't. It couldn't be. The man was confused and mentally incapacitated, that's all. Maybe some Helena had been his wife, or his sister or daughter and Gabby resembled her. He had said she looked like his sister's husband. The old man must have approached her for some reason like that. He couldn't have meant Gabby's Helena.

Fixing her grip on her bag of groceries, Gabby stood still on the sidewalk, watching the two men guide the old stranger back to the abandoned SUV. "Take me to him. Now." The stranger's shout at the other two men carried back to her. "I must see George right now!"

They spoke softly to him, mumbled words not meant to be overheard, and helped the old stranger into the backseat, then quickly got in and rushed away.

Gabby shivered. It must be so difficult to be confused and forgetful. And to care for someone who suffered with those challenges.

Still, wasn't it odd that of all the people on the street, he'd singled out her?

It was. Very odd. And yet his Helena had to be someone else. After all these years, the odds of her being the same woman attached to Gabby were statistically off-the-charts impossible. Of course, the encounter had been a simple case of mistaken identity. Those men had no way of knowing her Helena. One looked too young to even have been alive then.

Thanksgiving was in three days. Maybe the encounter was

something mystical, like a spiritual wink from Heaven just greeting Gabby, wishing her a happy holiday.

Though such a wink hadn't happened before, it still seemed far more likely than those men running in the same circles as her Helena. Thugs in expensive suits were still thugs. Their paths and her's never would have crossed.

The matter settled in her mind, Gabby dismissed it and walked on, eager to get home to prepare her solo Thanksgiving feast.

CHAPTER ONE

Handel Security, Inc.
New Orleans, LA
Friday, November 27, 8:00 p.m.

> *Happy 5th Anniversary, Gabby. Good work.*

> — *PETER HANDEL*

GABBY READ the card clipped to a plastic spike in a fragrant bouquet of flowers. The squat, clear vase had been on the edge of her desk when she'd come in that morning. Now, the cold and rainy day had turned into a cold and stormy night, and she sat alone in the IT division of Handel Security, Inc., certain her boss's secretary, who surely ordered the flowers, had been the only one to recall today was Gabby's fifth anniversary with the company. Honestly, if not for the flowers, Gabby doubted she would have remembered. Her time at Handel Security, Inc., seemed far, far longer.

And she had no one to blame for that but herself. What

else could happen when you chose a career to please someone else and not because you loved the work?

Inhaling the sweet blend of floral scents, she stroked the petal of a lavender iris and endured a bitter pang of regret. The saddest part was that her plan hadn't worked. The attempt to find something she and her father could share through their work hadn't been any more successful than her other many attempts to forge a common bond with him. *Face it, Gabby. In his eyes, you'll always be worthless.*

An all-too-familiar ache tightened her chest. Having had years of practice, she buried it swiftly then glanced through the rain-speckled window at the blurred city lights and fixed her gaze on the Superdome.

It is what it is. She had accepted it, truly. She just had to keep reminding herself that she had accepted it and he would never value her at all. Resigned, she turned her attention to work and reached for her keyboard. One more task and Fitch, who worked the IT night shift, should arrive and Gabby would be done for the day. It couldn't come soon enough . . .

Half-an-hour later, she'd finished her daily report and minutes afterward, Fitch arrived. Soaked to the skin, he pegged his jacket on the wall-hooks lined in a row near the door. "It's crazy cold and wet out there," he said, dabbing at his round face with a paper-towel. Scraps of soaked paper stuck to his graying beard. "You run the sweep?" He smoothed his wet, wind-tossed hair. It sprang back, shooting out in every direction.

"I did, and I started the backup at 7:30 sharp." Peter Handel insisted on protocol consistency. About three times a week, Fitch ran ten to fifteen minutes late, which meant Gabby either started the backup for him or she suffered the fallout with him.

While they rarely physically worked simultaneously, the boss held Gabby ultimately accountable for all things IT.

That was a perk of being very good at your job. Having a talented if perpetually late co-worker was a minor drawback. As irritants go, that one was tolerable. Today, she had again covered for Fitch, but not to keep Peter Handel from getting riled up. It was past time he set Fitch straight. Simply put, Gabby felt magnanimous. The boss had sent her flowers—even if he didn't realize he'd sent them. The gesture was just another insignificant protocol to him, but it was significant to her. In her world, thoughtful and kind gestures from others were both significant and rare.

"Whew! Thanks, Blake." Fitch slid onto his desk chair and then scanned his monitor. His jeans were wet from the knees down. "Peter would have docked my pay." Fitch tapped at his keyboard. "I've got the controls . . . now."

Biting her tongue, Gabby glanced at her own screen and confirmed the transfer. "Acknowledged." Looking forward to a hot meal and a long bath, Gabby logged off the system, then reached into her desk drawer and retrieved her handbag.

As she shut the drawer, her desk-phone rang. Praying it wasn't an internal or client problem Fitch couldn't handle, she answered. "IT, Gabby Blake."

"Miss Blake." The man's voice was vaguely familiar. He sounded weary and tense. "This is Dr. Abe Adams at Tulane Medical."

Neither he nor Tulane were established Handel clients. Either could be new, she supposed, and she just hadn't yet gotten the paperwork. Wait . . . Dr. Adams. She'd seen him in the ER last spring when she'd taken a tumble in the parking garage downstairs. "Of course, Dr. Adams. What can I do for you?"

"There's no easy way to say this, so I'll just spit it out. I do have a duly signed HIPAA release authorizing me to discuss this matter with you."

A HIPAA release? That confused her. "What matter is that, Dr. Adams?"

"Your father was brought in on a 911 call," Dr. Adams said. "He's had a stroke."

Her heart beat hard and fast. Her father? "Is he . . .?"

"He's alive and stable," Dr. Adams said quickly. "There's some paralysis on the right side of his body and his speech has been impeded, but he is writing a little now with his left hand, so we are able to communicate with him."

"What's he written?" Did he want her there, or not want her there? Considering he'd kept his emotional distance her whole life, she couldn't imagine he would want her to even know about this. To actually let her see him vulnerable? He'd hate that.

Dr. Adams ignored her question and asked one of his own. "Could you tell me, please? Who is Helena?"

Hearing her name spoken aloud stunned Gabby. Never, not once in all her life, had her father ever uttered the name in Gabby's presence. "Helena is . . . was my mother."

"Was? So, she's deceased then?"

"Yes, twenty-eight years ago. She died in childbirth when I was born." Long familiar pangs of guilt ripped through Gabby and she shifted on her seat.

"I see. May I ask if your father speaks of her often?"

"To my knowledge, he never speaks of her." Gabby stiffened. According to Janelle, the aunt Gabby had met once in her life at age twelve, her father didn't blame Gabby for her mother's death. He just couldn't stand to look at her because of it. *Some losses run too deep to forget.* "What is it you need from me, Dr. Adams?"

"Your father wrote down your name and phone number."

Which told her nothing. She worried her lower lip, ignored Fitch's slanted curious looks. He was clearly listening and pretending not to hear. She dropped her voice. "Why?

What does he want from me? Should I come to the hospital, or is he just letting me know?"

"Excuse me?"

No way could she say that again. The words would clog her throat and she'd choke. She opted for silence instead.

"You're his daughter, Miss Blake."

"I'm acutely aware of that, Doctor." She swallowed hard, tempered her tone. "Will he recover?"

"We believe he will. The first twenty-four hours were most dangerous, but he made it through them without further incident."

"The first twenty-four hours?" Surprise streaked up her spine. "When did this incident happen?"

"Three days ago," Dr. Adams said. "He was unconscious on the sidewalk—on Canal Street near the river. A passerby spotted him and phoned 911. Until today, we didn't know who to call. He's been writing, but until this evening, we couldn't decipher anything beyond the name, Helena. Confusion is common in these cases."

Apparently, Gabby wasn't an ICE contact in his phone or wallet, or they had been stolen. "He arrived without any iden-tification, then?"

"That's correct."

Stolen. "And his left side is impacted as well as his right?"

"Not from our testing, no. Just the right side."

"Dr. Adams, my father is left-handed," she said, cupping her forehead in her hand, her elbow atop her desk. "Why is his writing undecipherable?"

"After the trauma of a stroke, it can take time for the, er, confusion to dissipate. He's actually doing well on that front," the doctor assured her. "Has he had any illnesses or stroke symptoms in recent months? Slurred speech, the inability to form and speak complete sentences, or an inability to smile?"

Smile? Her father? Not likely. At least, not around her. "I don't know."

"Um, Miss Blake," Dr. Adams hesitated, then went on. "I don't want to pry, but have you been estranged? You and your father, I mean."

She slid Fitch a covert glance, but his chair stood empty. Relieved at his stepping away from his desk and giving her a little privacy, she blew out a long breath. "We're blood strangers, Dr. Adams," she said. "We have been since my birth." Forcing the pain of that fact out of her voice and infusing it with a strength she didn't feel took effort. "I'll come to the hospital if you like, but it would be prudent to first be sure he wants me there . . . for both our sakes. "

"I understand." The doctor softened his voice. "May I ask how long it's been since you've seen him?"

Her face went hot. "Christmas." An hour in a room together not talking, not looking at each other, was about all either of them could take. A knife couldn't cut through the tension. It'd be a challenge for a machete.

"Oh, you live away." Dr. Adam's voice lightened. "I'm sorry, Miss Blake. I thought you lived in New Orleans. The area code—"

"I do live in New Orleans," she admitted. "You weren't mistaken."

"But it's weeks until Christ . . . Oh, you meant last yea—" He stopped himself. "My apologies, Miss Blake." A long pause stretched into silence. Finally, he said, "I've sent a nurse to specifically ask your father if he wants to see you. She'll return momentarily." He cleared his throat. "Um, actually, with this virus, we wouldn't consider permitting you entry into the facility—it's patients only—but with no identification, we do need a positive ID. Ah, she's back now, and she's nodding." The doctor listened, then repeated. "She asked, and he wrote, 'Now'."

Now. That stunned Gabby. "Very well."

Dr. Adams hesitated. "You'll come to the hospital, then?"

"Of course." She glanced at the window. Huge raindrops splattered against the glass and ran in rivulets down the panes like rivers of tears. "Give me fifteen minutes."

"Thank you, Miss Blake. Masks are required, and I personally recommend gloves as well."

"Fine." Gabby hung up the phone. Her stomach fluttered. She demanded it stop and issued herself a stern warning: *Don't make anything out of this. He isn't going to suddenly become the dad you always wanted when he's never been the father you needed. People aren't built that way.*

Fitch returned to his desk with a steaming cup of coffee. "Hey, everything okay, Blake? Sounded like bad news."

"Everything's fine." She nodded in Fitch's general direction and walked toward the door, grabbing her coat and umbrella from the hook on the way. "Night."

Now. Adian Blake wanted to see her now. Why? Never in her life had he wanted to see her.

But never in his life had he looked into the face of death.

That could make a person want to see anyone familiar, even the only living relative he'd tried to ignore her whole life. Couldn't it?

She pushed the elevator button. If he still thought he was dying, then maybe. But surely he had been told he should recover.

Confused and conflicted, she stepped into the elevator, then pushed the down button to the parking garage. The descending motion conspired with her upset and her stomach lurched. She smoothed it with an unsteady hand, absolutely refusing to let his treatment of her make her feel inferior or unworthy. She'd been down that road most of her life and had yanked herself off it. She wasn't going there again.

The elevator door creaked open. Stepping out, she cut

through the rows of parked cars, passing right by her own vintage Mustang. Even with the rain, walking the few blocks to the hospital would be quicker than driving. Safer, too. Rain brought out the worst in downtown drivers.

What could he possibly want?

Her knees went weak. *Stop it, Gabby. Stop thinking. You don't have the answers. You never have had the answers for anything to do with him. Just follow the drill. Suck it up, stuff it down, and get to the hospital.*

Lightning flashed a jagged streak in the night sky. Thunder crackled and rolled, echoing between the tall buildings, and Gabby stepped outside, into the crazy cold and rain.

On the sidewalk, she hugged the overhangs to stay out of the sharp wind. Raindrops stung her skin through her coat. No wonder Fitch had come in soaked. If the rain kept up, pouring down in bucketsful, the streets would flood.

At the corner of Perdido and LaSalle, a VIP alert pinged her mobile. She fished her phone from her handbag and spotted a new text from Shadow Watcher.

Rushing across the street, Gabby ducked into the row of concrete archways built into the first story of an office building, and then read the message.

TROOP CALL. Amber Alert issued on Cally Jean Smith. 13. Birmingham, AL. Stranger abduction. She's in extreme danger, troops. Need all hands on deck. You know the drill. Time to suck it up and stuff it down.

Mist whipped in through the open arches and gathered on Gabby's face. She shielded her phone with a cupped hand. Two of the six Troop Search and Rescue members replied, then Gabby responded. "Gate Keeper OOC," she whispered as she keyed in the acronym for out of commission. "Sorry, SW. Medical emergency. Call in backup."

Another ping followed immediately. A private text to her from Shadow Watcher. "You hurt, GK?" she read.

She keyed in her response. "My father. Stroke. Headed to hospital now."

"You do what you need to do there. We've got this. Prayers are with you and your dad."

Dad? Gabby's throat constricted. Her father had never been a dad. She couldn't imagine him in that role. In a sense, that's what had led her to join the Troop Search and Rescue with Shadow Watcher five years ago. She had no family. No friends. No home life or support system or anyone to rely on. She had work. A job she was grateful for and good at, but it was work she didn't enjoy. And she needed more. Wanted more. What more, she didn't know, but something . . .

At her computer one night, she'd gotten an Amber Alert and decided to use her computer skills to help look for the child. She noticed the Troop Search and Rescue group and they noticed her noticing them. They watched each other but didn't interact until Gabby found a live feed of the missing girl and her abductor. The group always sent their data to Shadow Watcher, so she forwarded her sighting find to him, too. He took it to the authorities, and they found the girl. Safe. Returned to her mother alive.

Gabby had been elated, and for the first time in a long time, (*if ever* was too brutally honest to admit even just to herself), she felt connected and fulfilled. She had found a purpose.

In the weeks that followed, they found another child, and then another. Finally, Shadow Watcher messaged Gabby and formally invited her to join Troop Search and Rescue. They'd been seeking missing kids ever since.

Everyone in Troop Search and Rescue retained their

anonymity and everyone had an assigned role. Shadow Watcher collected data from the investigators, compiled and disseminated it to the appropriate authorities. Gabby was the Gate Keeper, keeping watch and covering the group's backs. The other four troop members, ThumpIt, Ferret, Hunter and TreasureSeeker, were investigators with different special skills. Whenever human traffickers were involved and exposed, the risks to the group exploded. So far, Gabby had kept their digital footprints light, masked and their identities protected. "Thanks, SW." She typed in her text and got a quick response.

"Let me know how it's going. If you need anything, yell."

"I'm fine." She answered by rote. "Thanks again."

"That's not lip service, okay? I mean it."

Gratitude spilled warmth into her. She didn't even know his real name and he still reached out to her in ways no one else ever had. Afraid if she shared anything more, she'd blubber like a fool, she limited her response to an emoji smiley face, then added, "GK going dark."

For some reason, breaking the connection to Shadow Watcher proved difficult. Her finger hovered above the screen, and she had to make herself tap Send. Absurd, really. She had never relied on anyone else. Yet as distant as the anonymous relationship was, a bond existed between them. Within Troop Search and Rescue, they worked most closely together online, and she innately trusted him. At least, more than she trusted anyone else, which honestly wasn't saying much. It was kind of crazy really, considering she knew nothing about him. She wasn't even a hundred percent sure he was a man, though he came across as a man in his approach and in the way he phrased and framed things. The other group members used the male pronoun to and about him, not that any of them had actually met him, either. But her feelings toward him . . . he had to be a guy.

Grateful she had been spared from explaining her relationship with her father for the second time that night, she stashed her phone, whispered a quick prayer for his recovery and then prayed Troop Search and Rescue found Cally Jean Smith and returned her home to her parents safe and sound.

How disappointing that only now have you prayed for your father, but a child you've never met, you pray for immediately.

Gabby rebutted the prick at her conscience. Cally Jean was a child and in extreme danger. He was an adult and getting professional care.

He's your father.

Boom. Got her on that one. Gabby sighed and kept walking. She should have prayed for him right away. Guilt swam through her. It wasn't that she didn't want to pray for him; she often did. It was him wanting her to come see him *now* that surprised her so much. His summons knocked her back on her heels and she still hadn't recovered her balance. She didn't know what to do with all the emotions it conjured.

Stop thinking, Gabby. Start there. She clenched her jaw. *Just follow the drill. Suck it up, stuff it down, and get to the hospital.*

"Right." She stepped through the last open arch back out into the driving rain. "Right."

CHAPTER TWO

Tulane Medical Center
8:30 p.m.

A NURSE from the station escorted Gabby down the hall and then into her father's room. Seeing him looking so frail and far older than his sixty years shocked her into clenching her hands. His skin looked as gray as his hair, which was tousled, and the right side of his face drooped. Her eyes burned and her throat went tight. What she had expected, she wasn't sure, but this . . . wasn't it. He looked old and fragile and—

"I'll let Dr. Adams know you're here." The nurse sent Gabby a reassuring look, then left the room and closed the door.

The silence was deafening. Gabby wasn't sure what to do, and for the millionth time, she wished just once things between them could be easy.

Her father pushed at the sheet and blanket covering him, working his left hand free. His hospital gown slipped down on his shoulder, but it was his hand that had his attention. He stared at it.

Gabby followed his gaze. He held a piece of paper clenched in his fingers. Her name had been scribbled on it. "Do you want me to read that?" she asked. When he nodded, she reached for the paper, her hand trembling, then read the words.

"Help me."

Bewildered, an odd uneasiness rippled through her and turned the taste in her mouth bitter. Their gazes locked. "Help you with what?"

No answer.

"Do you need the nurse?"

He tried but couldn't answer. The words refused to form.

"Blink once for no, twice for yes," she said. "Can you do that?"

He blinked twice.

"Do you need the nurse?"

One blink.

"The doctor?"

One blink.

She studied her father's angular face, then his eyes and doubted her own. Fear burned in their depths. She'd never before seen her father afraid. "Are you in pain?"

One blink.

"I know you're frightened," she whispered, stepped closer to his bedside. "You are, aren't you?"

He blinked twice.

Okay, that was progress. Surprised he'd admitted that much, she pushed for more. "Of dying?"

Two blinks.

Normal under the circumstances, and she could offer him some reassurance. "The nurse told me you're stable," Gabby said, inching a little closer still. "And Dr. Adams expects you to recover so—"

He interrupted her with a series of fast blinks.

What was he trying to tell her? She gave herself a second, then began again. "You're not afraid of another stroke."

One blink.

Why that terrified her, she couldn't say, but it did. "Did more happen to you than the stroke?"

He gave her a wide-eyed stare.

Not a yes or a no, which meant *what?* "You're afraid something more will happen to you? Something not related to the stroke?"

Two blinks.

Each one hit her like a ton of bricks. "Are you afraid someone is going to try to hurt you?" With his business associates, that likely was a fear he lived with all the time.

He hesitated as if torn between revealing his thoughts and not revealing them.

"You are," she guessed. "You're afraid someone is going to hurt you."

Wide-eyed, not agreeing or disagreeing. Something close but different. Something not personal . . . After she'd graduated college and moved to her apartment in the Garden District, he'd taken an early retirement from his job in lieu of being laid off. The company had been upper-level management heavy and he'd volunteered to go. He'd started a little company, keeping books for elite heavyweights. Though they paid well, many had shady reputations. She'd advised him against getting involved with them, especially with George Medros, the worst of the bunch, but only in her mind. Not that her relayed spoken opinion would have mattered to her father anyway. "Is this about your business?" she asked.

Two blinks.

"You're afraid one of your clients will hurt you?"

Two blinks.

"Why?"

No response.

She grappled with the disclosure, trying to puzzle it all out. "You're hardly a risk to any of them."

One blink.

The hair on the back of her neck lifted. "You are a risk?"

Two blinks.

Spotting a notepad on his tray-table, she held it so he could write and put the pen in his hand. "Tell me why."

He avoided her eyes and scrawled a few words. "Know 2 much."

The reason for his fear became abruptly clear. Diminished capacity and too many secrets. It made sense. The weight of having enemies like George Medros settled heavily on her shoulders. "What can I do?"

He pointed to the first note. *Help me.*

"How?"

With his index finger, he pointed at her, scratched the pen to paper, then showed her. "Do my work."

Her scalp tingled, and the sensation slithered down through her whole body. He was aligned with every crook in the parish, and he wanted her to do his work? He feared they'd hurt him, so he wanted her to cover for and protect him? Knowing not one of them would hesitate to hurt her.

Oh, God, this is so unfair. She squeezed her eyes shut.

When she reopened her eyes, he pointed to another note he'd scribbled. "Go. Think. Come tomorrow."

"Do you want police protection?"

One blink.

She nodded. "All right. I'll be back after work tomorrow."

He raised his hand and shooed her, let out a garbled, "Go."

So, he willingly puts her life in jeopardy and then shoves her away. Gabby stiffened her back, chiding herself for being even mildly surprised, and then left the room and closed the door.

The nurse who'd escorted her in seemed surprised to see her in the hallway. "You're leaving?" She frowned. "But Dr. Adams . . ."

Gabby didn't slow her steps but hastened them, moving toward the elevator. "Tell him I've been dismissed."

CHAPTER THREE

GABBY WALKED BACK to her office for her car. By the time she trudged through the downpour to the parking garage housing her Mustang, the water on the streets stood ankle-deep. The short drive to her Garden District apartment was treacherous and, when she finally arrived, her shoes were wrecked and she was more drenched than Fitch had been. And freezing cold. Opting for warmth over food, she skipped dinner and headed straight for a long, hot bath.

Soaking up to her neck in the deep tub, she couldn't keep her mind out of overdrive. What exactly had her father meant? *Help me? You do my work?* Stuffing down feelings of betrayal, of his willingness to cost her everything, she tried to bury the potential impact of his request on her and center her focus on his issues. *Which client, which work had him so afraid?*

Maybe he was just confused. Her heart preferred confusion over his sacrificing her and her future and reputation, his betrayal and his disregard for putting her in jeopardy. His neurons could be misfiring and everything in his brain be jumbled. Yet he hadn't come across as jumbled. He had very clearly tagged work as his worry and flatly denied his health spurred his fear. That meant he was either more than confused—who wouldn't be worried sick after a debilitating stroke? —or he'd been threatened by one of the shady characters he called clients. Had someone threatened to kill him?

The truth struck her way down deep. It would take something that bad for him to turn to her for help.

Too agitated to stay in the water, she toed the drain plug, emerged, dried off and slipped into a knee-length t-shirt, then headed to the kitchen. Over the years, she'd overheard him on the phone often enough to know he knew better than to associate with those kinds of people. When he'd taken them on as clients, it had struck her as completely out of character. She had studied her father from a distance her whole life and she never had known him to cross the line between right and wrong. So why had he aligned with them?

She hadn't been able to make sense of that at the time, and she couldn't now.

After filling the tea kettle and setting it on the stove to heat, she retrieved a jar of Earl Grey White Tip tea from the cabinet. Maybe she was wrong. She spooned four teaspoons into the teapot, then reached into the cabinet for a cup. Maybe he was like them, and he did a superb job of hiding it. That pretense would be easy short-term, but long-term? Not so much.

The kettle whistled.

Gabby poured the boiling water into the teapot, inhaled the aromatic steam. Or maybe he'd panicked at being forced into early retirement and had done the first thing he could find to make decent money. But if he'd had money problems, she didn't know about them. She'd never noticed anything like past due bills in the mail, or food being short in the fridge, or anything to suggest he wasn't financially secure. Yet considering the strain in their distant relationship, would she notice? Would he permit her to notice? Not then, and certainly not now that she wasn't living under his roof. He could be wealthy or nearly broke and she'd have no idea. That's the way he not only wanted it but had insisted it be her whole life.

When the tea had steeped, she filled her cup, snagged it and her phone, and then curled up in her favorite living room chair near the front window. *Let it go. You'll never figure him out. Just suck it up, stuff it down, and wait until tomorrow. He'll tell you what he wants you to know then.*

Good advice but easier said than done. His fear was real. And though they were strangers, they were blood.

Make yourself crazy then.

No, she needed to think of something else. Someone else. Shadow Watcher came to mind and stayed. He was the closest thing to a friend she had, and he was just shy of a stranger. Outside the thunder moved closer, the relentless storm seeming to gather in intensity. Unfortunately, it mirrored the storm building within her. *Do something.*

She texted Shadow Watcher. "Any luck finding Cally Jean Smith?"

"Not yet," he responded. "We have a fresh lead. Possible sighting in Huntsville. Troops are checking it out. How's your father?"

"The doctor says he's stable."

"But?"

She wanted to tell him. To talk over the situation. But she'd never before confided in anyone else. Well, aside from her aunt, Janelle. Just once Gabby had spoken openly to her mother's only sister and look how that had turned out. She'd come to New Orleans, given Gabby a book of recipes for handmade soaps and lotions and oils that once had belonged to her grandmother, promised she'd bring Gabby to her home in New York for a summer visit, and never had been heard from again.

Gabby still had no idea what she'd done wrong to keep her aunt from returning. But she'd learned the lesson of keeping her issues to herself. She didn't have much of a relationship with Shadow Watcher, but she wasn't willing to risk losing it by dumping her problems on him to discuss. "I'll know more tomorrow," she said, equally determined not to lie.

"Stable is good. Is he talking?"

"No, but he's writing a little."

"Complaining or doing the drill-sergeant routine?"

She smiled in spite of herself. "He didn't complain to me."

"GK is being evasive. How unlike you."

"SW is pushing, knowing all the troops have identity issues." Remaining anonymous wasn't just important. It was critical to their well-being.

"Sorry. Didn't mean to pry. Just concerned."

Shadow Watcher was concerned. About her. Her heart warmed. "Thanks. I'm fine."

"GK, whenever you say you're fine, you're never fine. You're worried. Save the canned answers for those who don't know you."

She grunted. "Must I remind you that you don't really know me?" She hit Send then sipped at her tea.

"Maybe we've never met, but I know you. You work too hard, you fully commit to what you do, you have no one else and you have a tough relationship with your father. In five years, you've mentioned him less than ten times—usually when you're seeing him at Christmas and on his birthday, which you did not do last year. The birthday, I mean. You saw him Christmas."

He'd noticed all of that? "I sent him a birthday cake. I just didn't visit."

"Didn't know about the cake. Did know you hadn't seen him."

Curious. "How did you know I hadn't seen him?"

"You weren't tense for a week. Whenever you see him, you're as tight as stretched wire for a week either side of the visit."

Was she? She sipped from her tea and set her cup on the side-table coaster, then shrugged. She was. "I knew you were observant but not this observant."

"Oh, you'd be surprised. When I'm interested, nothing escapes me."

And he was interested in her? She must have misunderstood. That's what he had said, but it couldn't be what he'd meant. "Are you saying you're interested in me?"

"Of course."

Her heart slammed against her ribs. A bolt of panic and a reed of excitement too pleasant to accept as honest shot through her, confusing and anxiety-inducing. "Why?"

"It's complicated."

Evasive? That was odd. "I asked why?"

"At first, because you found Troop Search and Rescue. We don't get found. I didn't trust you. So, I watched you, and you were sharp. And really skilled. I wanted to know how skilled, so I kept watching. You can't deny your talent is impressive, GK."

So was his. "You said, 'at first'."

"I did."

Typical. Not giving an inch. She pushed. "That implies your reasons changed."

"They did."

She grumbled under her breath. "To what?"

"Honestly?"

"Always."

"Okay, then. Fascination. You are different from most women."

That could be a good or a bad thing. If bad, she didn't want to know it. Not now. Gate Keeper was specifically gender neutral. How had he figured out she was a she? Since asking would be counter to her interests, she changed the subject. "You asked what my father wrote. It was just two words."

"What were they?"

"Help me."

"With what?"

"I'm not sure, but I suspect he's got some trouble going on in addition to his health issues." She made herself stop there, hoping she hadn't already said too much. "I'll know more tomorrow."

"Should I put Troop Search and Rescue on alert?"

"No, absolutely not. I'll handle it." At some point in their conversation, she'd decided to trust him a little, but rely on him? On the troops? No. That was too far out of her comfort zone to even contemplate.

"This is all tough stuff, GK. You don't have to go through it alone. I—we—are here for you."

Her eyes burned. The back of her nose stung. And the desire rising in her to empty her heart to him swept through her. Words she had suppressed her whole life fought to be spoken. She swallowed hard repeatedly, barely kept them unspoken and contained inside her. *Stuff it down! Stuff it down!* "That's very kind of you, but this is nothing I can't handle."

"You don't know that. You don't even know yet what help he needs."

Because she couldn't refute that, she changed the subject again. "How do you know I'm alone?" He knew she was a woman, too. "Have you investigated me, SW?"

"Simple logic. You never mention anyone else. Not even in passing. Everyone else does. Names withheld, but relatives and their issues come up. Everybody has issues, GK. But the only person you ever mention is your father, and that's only twice a year."

Side-stepping her question. Answering without answering. "You checked me out." Her mind jumped into high gear. "Before you invited me to join Troop Search and Rescue."

"I can neither confirm nor deny your allegation, but I can vow you've nothing to fear from me. I never tangle with a woman sharper than I am who wouldn't hesitate to rip me to shreds."

"Détente."

"Ah, good. So, will you admit now that you checked me out, too?"

She'd tried, of course. Met with limited success but gave it her every effort. Still, her face went hot. "I've looked at all our members, of course. It's my job. Can't cover someone's back or keep the bad guys on the outside of the gate if you don't know anything about them."

"Fair enough. Were you fascinated, too?"

Another odd response. And it ignited an even odder response in her. "SW, are you flirting with me? Because it appears you are and, if you are, I have to tell you, your timing is terrible."

"Maybe my timing is off, but you don't sound scared anymore. Your fire is back."

A smile curved her lips and she scraped her teeth over her lower lip. "Touché. And thanks." Definitely a guy reaction and way of handling things. Was the flirting just a distraction then? Highly likely. Her disappointment about that however was very real.

"Data incoming on Cally Jean. I expect an update from

you tomorrow on your father. Don't let me down, GK. I'm alone and need to feel needed, too."

She read, then re-read that last sentence half a dozen times, feeling the bond between them strengthen. "I won't let you down." Committing, she took the plunge. "You're not alone. I'm the Gate Keeper. I've got your back."

CHAPTER FOUR

Garden District
Monday, November 30, 9:00 p.m.

THE DAYS after the hospital summons passed in a blur of work, doctors and hospital visits. In piece-meal and, Gabby feared, half-truth revelations from her father about his situation. And in text messages with Shadow Watcher, trying to make sense of the puzzle pieces her father presented. Today, he had shocked her, dropping the entire puzzle right in her lap.

That night, in her cozy chair with her tea, she texted Shadow Watcher. "Free?"

"Waiting for you, actually. We've got good news. It's taken a lot longer than expected, but we located Cally Jean Smith last night. Less than twenty miles north of the Mexican border. Rescue op was successful. As of four o'clock this afternoon, she's back with her family."

Twenty miles. "Wow. That was close." If she'd crossed the border, the odds of ever finding her dropped to miniscule. "Is she okay?"

"Bruised and scraped but not physically violated. Docs say with time, she'll be fine."

The professionals would help her deal with the emotional scars. In cases like these, there were always emotional scars. They'd give her tools to help her cope constructively, and there was solace in that. "Wonderful news. Congratulate the troops."

"Will do. So, what's new on your home front?"

"Bombshell day." In a few days, she'd moved past withholding information from him. He seemed to always know what she didn't say anyway, and what she didn't bring up, he led her to reveal. Oddly, recognizing exactly what he was doing didn't bother her. It gave her a license to open up and talk about it. That was a luxury she'd never before had and, even more bizarre, she liked it. Talked about, the issues didn't seem as dark or overwhelming. "His doctor wants him out of the hospital—risks of contracting the virus—and he doesn't recommend rehab for the same reason, so my father is coming home shortly, but he can't take care of himself. I'm moving back in with him for a while. Keeping my apartment."

"Great for him. Not so good for you, considering. Wise, keeping the apartment. You'll need a refuge." Blunt and to the point, as usual. "How can you take care of him and work? Remote?"

"Remote isn't an option." Peter Handel wanted her on site and wouldn't bend on that. She couldn't blame him for not wanting Fitch loose and unmonitored much less in control. "I hired an angel, Lucy Mason. She's going to be with him when I'm not. She's a caretaker and physical therapist the doctor recommended."

"Did you run a check on this angel?"

"Briefly. Not much time. But she's well-trained, recommended and bonded."

"I'll go deep."

Shadow Watcher's brief checks outshone her deep background checks. He had a talent for them and access to places she couldn't go. How he'd gotten it, she had no idea and she had never asked. "Thanks."

"Anything new on exactly what he's afraid of?"

She'd already told Shadow Watcher about her father's one-man business and his clients being high-profile, shady and neck-deep in questionable deals. That he'd plop her in the middle of those activities had infuriated Shadow Watcher. What had happened today wouldn't sit well either. "His 'help me' mystery is finally solved." Why her father had dragged out telling her until the last minute was anyone's guess. He hadn't explained, and she'd wearied of asking him questions he steadfastly refused to answer. "Until he recovers, he wants me to run his business."

"He's deliberately involving you with thugs he fears want him dead? He's putting you front and center on George Medros's radar? Is he still confused or crazy?"

She couldn't fault Shadow Watcher for raising the very questions she'd wondered herself. George Medros was one of the biggest organized crime bosses in the State of Louisiana. One of the most ruthless, too. That flood-of-betrayal feeling returned, and she didn't bother trying to stop it. She'd failed repeatedly and just accepted her father was willing to sacrifice her to save himself. That truth, strangely enough, didn't at all shock her. He'd protected himself and his emotions her entire life. "Confused? No. Crazy? Probably, but so am I. I agreed to help him."

"No, GK. No way."

"Way. I'm doing it, SW." Gabby dug in her heels.

"Why? Knowing what you know, doing what you do, why would you get mixed up in any of this? You could lose everything, including your life."

Truth time. Did she dare? She didn't not dare, considering

Shadow Watcher's connections with authorities. "I have to help him. This is the first time he's ever looked me in the eye or asked me for anything. For the first time ever, he isn't pushing me away and keeping his distance. He finally isn't treating me as if I'm worthless." She paused, then added, "He needs me and my help. How can I refuse? Could you refuse your father?"

"My father isn't afraid his client's going to kill him," Shadow Watcher shot back. "I can't believe the man is dragging his only child into the middle of his mess. Think about that, GK."

Valid point. "I have thought about all of it. But if I don't help him, he'll lose everything he's worked for his whole life. He'll have nothing."

"If he's dead, he won't need anything. If you are, neither will you."

"And that's the point. If I help him, he won't be dead. I can do what needs doing in a couple of hours each night. No one will know he isn't doing the work himself, so I won't be in jeopardy." She omitted disclosing her father insisting on that, citing his need to avoid his clients having a confidence crisis. He didn't mention the potential conflict of interest doing his work created for her at Handel. Peter Handel would fire her in a heartbeat.

Had her father even thought about that? Unsure, the possibility he hadn't grated on her. But, either way, she wouldn't turn her back on him. She'd been waiting for this chance forever. Surely, this would create the father-daughter bond she'd hungered for her entire life. Surely, it would.

"Look, GK. I get it. You think maybe this will bring you two closer together."

"Maybe we'll finally be family. Do you know what it's like to never have that, SW? To be almost strangers with your one parent and to have no one else?"

"Honestly, no, I don't. I'm alone not because I don't have family, but because I keep a lot of secrets from them. Have to, with what I'm doing. But that doesn't change the facts. He is putting you at risk. I have a bad feeling about this, and that's the truth."

"You're afraid I'm going to be disappointed and hurt."

"I'm afraid you're going to be dead or crushed and in a bad mood for a lot longer than a week either side one of your visits to him."

"I probably will be crushed," she admitted. "Emotionally, anyway. Odds are against anything else, but if there's a chance —even a small one—I have to take it."

"And that admission is one of the things about you that fascinates me."

He fascinated her, too. He had since the beginning, but this week . . . He somehow made all of the upset and uneasiness in her life easier to shoulder. At first, she thought that was because she was actually talking with him about personal matters. But she'd come to accept the reason went deeper. He was on her side. She'd never before had anyone on her side like this. There was strength in it.

Oh, Shadow Watcher still came across as blunt and brusque, but he was caring and blunt and brusque, softening, and so was she. The walls around her life, guarding her privacy and keeping others at arm's length were crumbling. At least where he was concerned. Not that her initial reaction about her father putting her at risk had been unlike Shadow Watcher's. It'd been exactly like his reaction. Still, this chance to bond . . . she had to take it. Her hungry heart, the neglected child inside, the isolated woman facing the world alone, insisted on it. She'd talk Shadow Watcher around eventually. "Really, I'm not expecting a miracle. But I am going to hope, SW." It took a lot for her to admit that. "God works in mysterious ways."

"You hope then. Me? I'll pray he doesn't get you both killed."

An icy shiver coursed through her. Clearly, Shadow Watcher understood the stakes.

Friday, December 4, 7:45 p.m.

JUST BEFORE MIDNIGHT on the eve of her father's hospital release, Shadow Watcher had reported back that the angel hired to help care for Gabby's father, Lucy Mason, was squeaky clean. She'd never had a passport, had no priors—not even a traffic ticket—and like many in New Orleans, she was a devout Catholic who attended morning mass daily and had done so for years. "No one's slate is *that* clean," Shadow Watcher had warned Gabby. "I'm going to keep digging."

And he had kept digging, but reportedly had found nothing, which worried him and amused Gabby. Dogs with their bones had nothing on Shadow Watcher when he was on a mission. He never quit, and he refused to let go.

What beyond Lucy's ultra-clean living had triggered his instincts, Gabby had no idea. But in the past, when Shadow Watcher had been triggered, something had eventually turned up. That fact niggled at Gabby and kept her on guard.

Release-Day morning passed quickly at work, and in the afternoon, Gabby retrieved her father from Tulane and took him home. Shadow Watcher still hadn't dug up any dirt on Lucy, so he finally warmed to the idea of giving Gabby an all-clear with *almost* no reservation. His *almost* all-clear of course included a keep-a-close-watch advisory. That was pretty good for a man who never backed off an instinctive warning in his life, and it helped soothe Gabby's concerns.

She'd been on her own for five years and out of her

father's house. The idea of moving back into it and getting involved in his work had her nerves plenty raw. Lucy summed up their situation in short order and, giving her credit, she didn't seem fazed by it. Actually, she made an excellent buffer between Gabby and her father.

The first three days went well. Work, then home to a hot meal. Her father remained in his room for his protection from the virus. Important with Gabby and Lucy interacting with others. A quick check on him each evening through his bedroom door, and that had been that.

But this was day four, Friday night actually, and it would be different. A challenge. It would be Gabby's first night doing Adian Blake's work, and they were to start in on it immediately after dinner. Lucy would place a chair in the hallway and from his bed, he could brief Gabby through the door on the work to be done.

Gabby had been on edge about that briefing since lunch. By the time she was ready to leave the office, she was a bundle of nerves and delaying her departure. Once she opened the first file on his work, she couldn't go back. She wasn't sure she would be able to meet her own eyes in the mirror. Was a long-elusive father-daughter bond worth a woman's integrity? Forfeiting her self-respect? Normally, it would not be. But the starved child in her craved acceptance. Craved approval. Honestly, she craved love.

Living a life never having been loved by anyone created a potent force. A chance to change that demanded all. Nothing else in life had proven as strong as that need and desire. Everyone should be important to someone. To just one someone . . .

Gabby parked her car in the drive then tucked her keys into her handbag. Outside the front door of her father's house, she stopped, her hand on the doorknob, and took in three long, deep breaths to steady herself. Expelling the last one, she twisted the knob. The door creaked open.

Unlocked? Gabby frowned. Lucy kept the door locked. It'd been locked every other night. Why wasn't it locked now? Gabby's stomach sank. Every nerve in her body went on alert. She pushed the door open wider. Dark inside, she called out. "Lucy?"

No answer.

Some instinct kept Gabby's feet firmly on the front porch. She stretched to see deeper into the house. Not a single light burned. Even the lamp in the entryway, which typically stayed lit around the clock, was off. Gabby's alarm deepened. Dread washed through her. "Lucy?" she called out again.

Still no answer.

Reaching into her purse, Gabby pulled out her pepper spray then reached for the wall switch and turned on the overhead light. The lamp stood undisturbed in its place on the entry table. Maybe the bulb had just burned out. Chiding herself for overreacting, she stepped inside.

Light from the entry streaked across the carpeted floor and she got a view of the living room. Total disarray. Gabby clicked on the light and scanned the mayhem. Every sofa cushion lay askew, shredded. The glass-topped tables had been turned upside down, legs up in the air, the sculptures once atop them haphazardly littered the floor. Even the wall paintings hadn't escaped. Every framed canvas hung crooked, as if someone shoved at them to peek behind. *What had happened here? Had her father suffered an adverse reaction to a medication and gone into a rage? Had he driven Lucy over the edge?*

The dining room was in the same shape as the living room. Gabby called out again, headed into the kitchen. "Lucy?"

Every cabinet door stood open. Flour and sugar dusted

38

the floor, the empty bags discarded near the table. Broken plates and glasses had been left on the granite countertops; shards spilled over onto the planked-wooden floor. The spice rack stood empty, all its jars in a broken heap on the floor. The stovetop was bare. Whatever happened had happened before Lucy began preparing dinner.

Gabby stilled, listened, her heart beating faster and faster, echoing in her ears, throbbing in her temples. Eerie silence. No sounds except the dull drone of the refrigerator, the quiet whir of the central heating.

Her pepper spray ready to discharge, she edged room to room, scraping her back against the dimple-textured wall, turning on lights and visually scanning every inch of destruction. In the laundry room, half-dry towels draped across the open dryer door and the strong scent of chemicals hung in the dead air. Bottles of cleaning supplies had been dumped; the empties tossed into the laundry sink. Otherwise the room was clear. Lucy's bedroom and bath. Tussled, but clear.

In the hallway, Gabby turned back to the far side of the house. Her throat felt too dry to swallow. His office. She hadn't checked his office. Or upstairs. No way was she going up there alone.

At the French doors to his office, a funny feeling swam through her. Gabby stopped and flipped on the light switch. The room flooded with light and, instinctively, she gasped and recoiled.

The office was a worse disaster than the kitchen. Papers strewn everywhere; all his files dumped from the cabinets. Everything moveable had been kicked over, shoved or slung. His chair cushions had been slashed, the back of the leather wingchair he favored, marred with jagged, gashed cuts. Stuffing poked and pulled out.

But the smell was a hundred times worse than the sight.

Iron, like her hands when she'd emptied her piggybank and rolled all those old coins.

Blood.

The roof of her mouth tingled, and her palms sweated. She stiffened all over, bracing herself, then stepped around the splintered remnants of a banker's bookcase, and looked behind the desk.

Face down on the floor lay her father.

Lucy lay crumpled beside him.

Burnished blood stained their backs—the source of the awful smell. And a butcher knife with a long black handle protruded from Lucy's wound.

Stunned, doubting her eyes, Gabby couldn't move or look away. A scream burned her throat. One that came from so deep within, if she let it out, she'd never be able to stop it. To bar its escape, she clasped her hand over her mouth. *Stuff it down! Stuff it down!* Shaking so hard she feared convulsing, Gabby forced herself to breathe, to bend, to check for signs of life.

There were none.

Get out of the house, Gabby. The killer could still be here. Get out!

She'd heard no sounds, sensed no presence, but that meant nothing. Quickly, she hurried to the front door and then down the sidewalk to the driveway, back to her Mustang. Fumbling her keys, she jerked open the car door and then checked inside. Empty. Scrambling in, she slammed and locked the doors. *Think, Gabby. Think.*

She needed help.

Now.

Finally gripping her phone, she dialed 911.

An operator answered. "Nine-one-one. What is your emergency?"

"My father and his caretaker have been murdered." Gabby darted her gaze to the house, across the lawn, and down the street. Quiet. Still. Nothing seemed odd or out of place. She answered the operator's questions, reciting the address and her name.

"Where are you now, Gabby? Are you still in the house?"

"Locked in my car."

"Good. You stay there. Officers are on the way. Don't you open the car-door for anyone else."

"Okay. Okay, thank you." Gabby hung up, hearing too late the operator instructing her to stay on the line. But she didn't call back; she needed her phone to text Shadow Watcher.

"My father was right. Just got home from work and found him and Lucy murdered. Police on the way." Gabby hit Send.

"Stuff it down, GK. First things first. Are you safe?" Shadow Watcher's words filled the screen on her phone.

He was there. *Thank you, God. Thank you.* "Locked in my car. Pepper spray in hand."

"How did it happen?"

"Stabbed. Lucy for sure, and my father, I think. No blood spray. No smell of gunfire. Just blood, and the knife in Lucy's back. Looking for something. Tore up everything."

"No signs of anyone else in the house now?"

"Didn't hear or see anyone. Everything is wrecked, SW. An elephant could be in there and I might not have seen it. I didn't go upstairs at all."

"Where did you find them?"

"In his office." Why was he out of bed? Downstairs? Why was he in his office?

"Together?"

"Yes."

"Clearly, Lucy wasn't a plant."

"Is that what you thought?"

"It is. But if so, she was double-crossed."

They texted back and forth a few more times, him getting

as many details down as she could recall. Then Shadow Watcher asked, "What was missing?"

"Who knows? I told you, the entire place was trashed."

"What about his computer? Was it there?"

She stilled. Clients. Computer. Why hadn't she thought of that? Summoning her frantic memories of what she'd seen in his office, she mentally scanned his desk. "No. It was gone. His external hard drive, too. He used it to store backups."

"Do you know what was on it?"

"Not a clue. He was going to show me some of his work tonight."

"You didn't have his password?"

"No, I didn't."

"And you didn't peek in—? "

"Hack my father? Absolutely not."

Sirens sounded in the distance and drew near. Gabby looked back over her shoulder and saw two police cars pull to the curb and stop. A third one joined them and then an unmarked car.

"Police are here. I have to go."

"I'll be close. Keep me posted."

"Thanks." She wished he were not close but with her. Still, if she'd had to wait alone . . . Her dry eyes burned. Tears hadn't yet come. They would. Of course, they would. But not now. Now, she had to hold herself together.

Her father had known this would happen. He'd known someone would murder him. Had he known that person would murder Lucy, too?

A rap sounded on her car window. "Miss Blake?"

A police officer in uniform, his badge clearly visible. Opening the door, she stepped out of the car. "Officer, my father is dead." Tears spilled down her cheeks. "He and Lucy, his caretaker, are both dead."

CHAPTER FIVE

Monday, December 7, 4:30 p.m.

"GK, ARE YOU THERE?"

Sitting at her kitchen bar, Gabby read the text message from Shadow Watcher and asked herself the same question. *Was she?*

She'd dealt with the police the night of the murder, spoken with Detective James Marsh, who'd been assigned the homicide case, and with Special Agent Andrew Bain, the FBI agent assigned, though no one had yet explained to her why the FBI was involved in the double-homicide case.

The potential Medros connection created priority status on processing the scene and in the coroner's office. Gabby had arranged for a graveside service for her father, which only she and two of his former co-workers had attended, and she had gone to Lucy Mason's funeral. Hundreds were there; her family devastated, ravaged by grief.

The contrast in the two services was stark and unnerving. And it made Gabby wonder. If she died, beyond an empty desk at her office, would anyone notice?

That inevitably led to her spending a lot of time thinking. Asking herself questions she maybe should have asked long ago. The one plaguing her now was particularly rough. Her insides felt clawed and shredded, ripped apart and trapped in the merciless clenches of regret and grief. If she'd been a different kind of daughter, would Adian Blake have been a different kind of father?

In the hours since returning home to her apartment, Gabby's mind tumbled as if caught up in a tornado's twisting winds. She doubted everything—her faith, her priorities, even herself. But sometime between three and four, totally overwhelmed and a breath from breaking down, she put all her fears and insecurities and regrets and wishes in God's hands. His vision was 20/20 on everything. Hers was too cloudy to trust at all, and she was flawed and rattled to the core. Staring at the phone screen, she repeated Shadow Watcher's question to her in her mind. *Was she there?*

She was. What there was of her and, at the moment, she just couldn't be sure exactly what that included. As odd as her grief might be, it definitely made everything seem worse.

Settled, she lifted her phone and answered Shadow Watcher's text. "I'm here."

"The funerals go okay?"

"About like funerals go," she texted back. "I'm glad they are done."

"I wish you had let me come with you."

He had offered. Multiple times. And she'd refused. Facing the funerals on her own, she could do it. She had faced everything in her life alone. But if he had been there with her, she would have leaned hard on him. Maybe. Probably, as messed up as she was right now. What would have happened then? She might have fallen apart. That was the thing about depending on someone else for anything. It made you weak and vulnerable. Then, when he drew back from her, where would she be? Alone again. Only this time, she'd know what she was missing. Know what it was like to have someone to lean on. No. No, she couldn't do it. She'd be a fool to put herself through that.

"You doing all right?"

How did she answer that? Was anyone who'd lost a parent on Friday all right on Monday? Okay, so they had been distant, nearly strangers. He had never been a dad. He hadn't wanted to be in her life or wanted her in his life. But they'd had a chance to bond—well, the start of a chance to bond— and now that was gone and so was he.

Being orphaned at any age is hard. When death robs you of your one chance to prove your worth, it's merciless. Constantly hammering your heart. "Yeah, I'm all right," she responded. Whether or not that was true, it was all she was capable of at the moment. "Agent Bain called. He's coming over with an update."

"Today? Are you up to that right now?"

Concerned. She felt Shadow Watcher's worry. "Considering the murderer is still out there, and I don't want to keep looking over my shoulder every second, yeah, I am fine with him coming now. The sooner, the better."

"Troop Search and Rescue sends its condolences, GK. Anything you need, anything at all, you just say the word. We're all on stand-by for you."

"Thanks." Moved, her throat thickened, and her chest tightened. "Settling his affairs won't be difficult. His lawyer's already been in touch and everything is in order. He did a full legal review a few months ago."

"Why?"

"Isn't that an interesting question? I can't answer it. Unfortunately, neither could his attorney."

"Fits in with your father's expectation someone would kill him, doesn't it?"

"It does," she admitted, then went on, grateful the words could be typed and certain she could never speak them. "It also confirms the stroke had nothing to do with the reason he felt that fear."

"Agreed. He's apparently worried about it for months, having the legal review. Are you thinking the stroke was induced?"

"Aren't you?" she whispered aloud while keying in her response.

The doorbell rang.

"Agent Bain has arrived. Will get back to you after he leaves." Her fingertip hovered above the Send button. Debating, she added, "Thanks for caring, SW."

"My privilege, GK. I'll be waiting."

Feeling a little less alone and despondent, Gabby stuffed her phone in the back pocket of her jeans on her way to the front door. She'd intended to change clothes before Agent Bain arrived, but messaging with Shadow Watcher had done her a lot more good. *Suck it up and stuff it down, Gabby.*

She checked the peephole and recognized the agent standing just beyond her door. He'd been with the NOPD homicide detective, James Marsh, the night of the murder at her father's house. Typical FBI black suit, white shirt and tie. Early forties, brown hair and nondescript, forgettable features. An asset in his line of work, she supposed. He'd removed his dark sunglasses, so she could easily identify him through the peephole.

Gabby twisted the deadbolt and then opened the door. "Agent Bain."

"Miss Blake." When she stepped back, he walked inside. "I'm sorry to intrude, especially with the funerals being today."

Funerals. Plural. He knew she'd attended Lucy Mason's

funeral as well as her father's. Gabby thought she'd seen him and Detective Marsh there, but honestly, she'd been absorbing so much in the stark difference between her father's funeral and Lucy Mason's, it was all a bit of a blur. Add her guilt about Lucy's murder, earned or not, and all the heartbroken grievers mourning Lucy, Gabby had been an internal wreck. But she had gotten through it all upright. That wasn't much, but it's what she had, so she held onto it tightly. "Come in and have a seat," she told Bain. "Can I get you something hot to drink?" It had been a chillingly cold day and the night had turned frigid.

"No, thank you." He walked over to the sofa but waited for her to sit down in her comfy chair before sitting. "I wanted to wait at least until tomorrow to get in touch, but there's been a development that made waiting imprudent."

Surprise rose and Gabby stiffened. "You've arrested the killer?"

"No, no. Sorry. We're still working on that," he told her. "Detective Marsh called with new information from a credible source, a confidential informant he's worked with for a good while."

The term was familiar to her. Troop Search and Rescue had used it for as long as she had been with them. "What did the CI report?"

"I can't independently confirm this, but Detective Marsh said word on the street is George Medros put out the contract on your father." The skin between Bain's thick brows bunched. "You know who he is, right?"

"Organized crime. Everyone in New Orleans knows who he is. What we don't know is why he isn't in prison."

"I've wondered the same thing, Miss Blake. It isn't for a lack of trying."

That, she understood. People like Medros had layers and layers of protection between them and their crimes. "And

Lucy? Was she contracted, too?" Gabby couldn't imagine it, but confirmation was warranted.

Bain's mouth twisted but his voice remained level. "Collateral damage."

Collateral damage? Anger simmered in Gabby, threatening to boil over. Lucy had been such a good woman, beloved by her family and friends, and these thugs had reduced her to collateral damage? She'd had dreams and purpose and a life.

Guilt swam through Gabby. If only she hadn't hired Lucy. If only she'd taken a leave of absence from work and been there herself, Lucy would still be alive. Gabby squeezed her eyes shut a long moment, struggled to get a grip on her emotions. *Stuff it down!* "How . . . tragic."

"Yes." The agent nodded his agreement, then laced his fingers atop his knee. "We suspect Medros feared his secrets wouldn't remain secret because of your father's mental condition."

"So, he mitigated his risks." Gabby absorbed and processed that. The stroke definitely had not been a stroke. It'd been a botched assassination attempt. "His people tossed my father's house, looking for Medros's information to make sure it didn't end up in your hands. Is that right?"

Bain's face turned red. "That's our suspicion." When she stared silently at him, he added, "Which the detective's CI affirmed."

Gabby followed Bain's line of thinking. "The computer and hard drive being taken substantiates your theory." Alone, it could also substantiate a muddied home invasion.

"It does, but it's not enough."

"No, it isn't."

Bain rubbed at the back of his neck. "Why would they toss the whole house? What else could they have been looking for?"

Gabby shrugged. "I have no idea. As I've explained, my

father and I were not close. I know next to nothing of his affairs and even less about his business practices."

Bain's facial expression remained passive, but determination hardened the look in his eyes. "When you were living at home, did he have friends who dropped by regularly?"

"No. He was very much a loner." She hadn't thought a thing of that at the time. It was just normal.

"No women in his life?"

"Not to my knowledge." Gabby never had seen one.

"Ever?"

"Ever."

"Strange." Bain focused on something beyond the far wall. "He was a young man when your mother passed. It's odd that he'd cut himself off from friends or companions like that."

It was strange. Of course, he could have met someone during the day or when he went away on trips or after she went to bed at night. She had no idea. "I can't speak to his reasons, Agent Bain. I just know I never saw another woman in his life. If there was one, I'm unaware of it."

"What about his work habits?"

"What do you mean?"

"Did he go to his home office every evening?"

"When I was growing up, he did." She thought back, pictured him in his chair beside the fireplace, which she'd never seen him light. It was just a dark, empty hole in the wall. "Mostly, he'd read."

"When he worked, did you see him make extra copies or anything like that?"

Bain thought he'd stashed backups somewhere in the house. "I didn't see anything like that. If I had, I wouldn't have known what he was doing." Clearly Bain had no idea what it was like to live with a distant father. She was glad he'd been spared, and she envied him his innocence.

"What do you think they were looking for then, in the rest of the house?"

"I have no idea." She'd been asking herself that same question over and over. But she had no answers. "Until his stroke, in the last five years, I'd seen my father nine times. I wish I could answer your questions, Agent Bain. I wish I could answer my own. But I honestly just don't know anything about him or his life."

Bain's look said he wasn't certain if he believed her.

Unless she wanted to sow more seeds of suspicion in him, she needed to explain. "Look, the truth is my father worshiped my mother. She died having me. So, it was my fault she was dead. My father and I lived in the same house until five years ago, but I didn't know him. He couldn't stand to look at me. He was there, but he avoided me. I had a roof over my head and food to eat. Otherwise, I was pretty much on my own."

"Who took care of you?"

Gabby lifted her chin. "I had a nanny until I started middle school, then it was just me. If I needed a doctor, I made an appointment. If I needed clothes, I had a card and a limit. I went and bought them."

"What about parent-teacher meetings?"

"I showed up. He didn't."

"And holidays? Birthdays and Christmas?"

She swallowed. "What about them?"

"Did you celebrate?"

This was utterly humiliating. "We sat in the same room together for an hour. We didn't talk, we didn't even look at each other."

"No parties or gifts?"

"No parties. Token impersonal gifts at Christmas."

"How about graduation? That's a huge milestone." Bain

said, looking for something, anything. "Did he go to your graduation?"

"No."

"Not for high school or for college?" Bain frowned. "Surely he went to your college graduation."

"No on both." She looked Bain right in the eye. "He was not there."

"I'm confused." Bain looked perplexed, and appalled. "He treated you like he did and yet, when he had the stroke, he had the hospital call you."

"Yes."

"I understand he asked you to help him."

"He did. Yes."

"So did you? Help him, I mean."

"No. The day he was to explain what help he needed, he was murdered."

"Then you have no idea what he wanted you to do, do you?"

"None."

Baffled, Bain sat silently a long moment, absorbing. "Growing up, you must have been very lonely."

She still was, though not so much as she always had been since joining Troop Search and Rescue. "Being alone has always been normal for me, Agent Bain. When something is normal, it's just normal. You don't know anything different."

"But your mother had a sister. Wasn't she there for you, growing up?"

"Janelle Reinhardt," Gabby said, realizing he'd been doing some homework on her family. "She lives somewhere in New York. I'm not sure exactly where. I only saw her once when I was twelve."

"Once—in your whole life?"

Gabby nodded. "She said she was coming back, but she never did." For months, Gabby had dreamed of going to her aunt's house for the summer. But summer had come and gone without a word from her. Rejected again, Gabby had put her aunt out of her mind.

Agent Bain nodded, then passed Gabby his business card. "The authorities have released your father's house. You're free to return to it. We don't think you're in any immediate danger—even the CI knew you and your father were estranged—so you should be safe. But keep your wits about you, just in case. And if you find anything of interest at the house, let me know right away."

Gabby took the card, mortified to have her personal life so exposed, and devastated because the truth humiliated her. *Unlovable.* "If I find anything even remotely of interest, you'll be the first to know." She hesitated, then asked, "What are the odds of actually finding and bringing the killer to justice?"

"Honestly?"

She nodded.

"We'll do our best, but you said it yourself. Medros is slick. He never gets his own hands dirty. Even if we found who took the contract, the odds of us connecting it back to Medros are slim to none."

Gabby frowned, all too familiar with his type from her work with Troop Search and Rescue. "And the contractor could be anybody from anywhere."

"Frankly, yes."

What more needed to be said? They had little hope of catching a contracted killer, and no hope of getting Medros. "I'm sure you'll do what you can." She offered the platitude because Bain clearly needed it. What a thankless job he had. Gabby didn't envy him after all. He too carried his burdens and, no doubt, his scars.

"We will do everything possible."

Lip service. Her heart cried for justice he couldn't offer, yet she couldn't expect more from him than he was capable of giving. A lifetime with her father had taught her the futility in that. Accepting it, she stood up. "Thank you, Agent Bain."

He took the hint and departed.

Gabby locked the door behind him then paced between it and the kitchen bar, empty, furious and sick inside. Sometimes life just threw too much reality at you. She'd felt vulnerable and fragile before Bain's visit. Now she felt even worse. She felt hopeless.

9:45 p.m.

"You still with Bain?"

The Shadow Watcher text coming through startled her. How long had she been sitting, staring out the window at nothing? Long enough for the night to grow still and quiet and darkness to settle in. She reached to the table at her elbow for her phone. "He's gone."

"You tied up with something or someone?"

"No."

"Taking it the meeting didn't go well."

"You'd be right." She paused, considered deleting the message, then hit Send and immediately regretted it. Only a fool wouldn't realize Shadow Watcher knew exactly who she was by now. The path from her father's murder and the news stories made it easy for him to figure it all out. "Looks like a contracted hit ordered by your favorite mobster."

"And the angel?"

"Collateral damage." Gabby's eyes burned. "That one is on me. Had I handled his care myself, she wouldn't have been there."

"Had he not gotten mixed up with bad people, he

wouldn't have been there," Shadow Watcher reminded her. "But what is, is. So, what's next?"

"I'm off all week. Tomorrow I'm going to start packing up the house. I'm selling it."

"Is there a rush? Maybe you should give yourself some time to think about it. You grew up there."

A normal person would feel that way, but her "home" had never been "normal" only normal for her. No sense in not being straight up about anything at this point. "I have never been happy in that house. Honestly, I've never felt comfortable in it. If I never had to see it again, I'd be just fine."

"Isolated." Shadow Watcher texted back. "I hate that, GK."

"Me, too. Always have, but like you say, it is what it is," she whispered as she texted. "I need a fresh start."

"I've got time off coming. Want some help packing it up?"

Did she? The offer overwhelmed her. The troops would all come if she asked. They'd drop what they were doing and help her. But she couldn't do that, ask them to put their own lives on hold to help her sort out her own. More importantly, Troop Search and Rescue was the one thing she had that wasn't tainted by her past and wasn't a wreck. She didn't want it messed up, too. It was her refuge. A place she felt valued and treasured and appreciated. Almost lovable. No way did she want to risk losing that. She had nothing else. Now, no one else. "No, but thanks, and thank the troops for me. I need to do this myself."

"Emptying the house requires heavy lifting."

"I've scheduled movers to handle that part. They'll put what I keep in storage until I decide what I'm going to do."

"GK, you're alone only because you want to be. We are here. I am here. Remember that. If you change your mind at any time, you let me know. Whatever you need."

Tears blurred Gabby's eyes. "That means more to me than you'll ever know, SW. Thank you."

Sniffling, she set the phone down on the table. How ironic is life? On the same day she buries the only member of her family she discovers, for the first time in her life, she is not alone . . .

Ironic and twisted.

CHAPTER SIX

Tuesday, December 8, 5:00 a.m.

GABBY AWAKENED AT DAWN, dressed in jeans, a deep brown sweater and sneakers, and then left the apartment. She stopped by the coffee shop for a Cinnamon Latte and snagged a Chipotle Chicken Panini sandwich for lunch. It'd save her a trip out to get something later. Then she drove over and parked the Mustang in her father's driveway, fished the house keys out of her handbag and finally let herself in through the front door, locking it behind her.

Emptying a house was not for the faint of heart. Emptying a house where you'd found your father and his care-taker's bodies was even harder.

The moving company had delivered ample boxes on Monday morning, which were neatly stacked in the living room against the wall. While Gabby worked steadily, she had barely made a dent in the upstairs. On edge about the murderer having gained access to the house already, she reminded herself often of Agent Bain's assurances she should be safe here, and of Marsh's CI being aware of her and her father being estranged.

Life was just full of irony and gut-punches. The one thing she'd hated all her life now had become her protection.

Stuffing that down, she turned her mind to the work. The guest room and two baths were done. Today, she planned to first tackle her old room or her father's bedroom. Neither appealed.

"Suck it up, Gabby," she told herself. Sipping at her coffee, she stowed the sandwich in the fridge. Her room first. Then his—after she'd had the morning to steel herself. She hadn't been in his room since . . . ever. It was an off-limits domain, and always had been. Even after his return from the hospital, she'd only knocked on his door and asked if he needed anything.

"No," he had answered. "Good night."

Being dismissed even then, she totally understood her reluctance to trespass into his private domain now. What else could she be, considering?

Dropping her handbag on the kitchen counter, she fished out her pepper spray and stuffed it into her left back pocket, then her phone into the back right one. Not because she felt threatened, but if two murders could occur in this house in the middle of the day once, a murder here could happen again, regardless of what Bain or Marsh's CI said. Daylight hadn't protected her father or Lucy. Shadow Watcher had been right. Being alert and staying alert was just using common sense.

Gabby taped up two boxes and then headed up the stairs. A short walk down the hallway, she stepped into her old room. Its closet doors stood open and the space was nearly bare. Spare pillows and blankets, and a small familiar floral box were stacked on the shelf above the hanging rod. Gabby pulled the box down and then removed its top and looked inside.

A clothespin reindeer she had made in Kindergarten. A Mother's Day card made in grammar school when she hadn't wanted anyone to know she had no mother. A silver pin she had received from a computer club she never had joined in high school. Annual school photos, and one of her accepting her diploma from high school and then another from college. Both taken by strangers.

Her heart twisted. Graduation days had been painful. All the other graduates had been surrounded by family. She'd stood apart, alone, and watched them. So many laughing people, proud parents, and so much shared joy. Many times in her life she had felt isolated, but never more so than on those two days. Well, except for Christmas. Every Christmas.

"Where's your folks, Gabby?" Charles Day, her science lab partner, had shouted out to her after the high school ceremony when families were meeting up with their students on the front lawn of the facility.

"Over there," she'd said. "See ya." She'd nearly run to her car to get away, had fist-sized knots in her stomach before she'd left the parking lot. And, she admitted it, tears blurring her eyes.

It was a full two weeks later before her father ever mentioned the event. He sat with his breakfast at the kitchen table, his face hidden behind his newspaper. Apparently, there was a mention of the graduation ceremony in the news because he asked her, "Did you graduate?"

"Yes."

"Are you going to college?"

"Yes. I start classes in two weeks."

"Where?"

"Tulane."

"I'll arrange funding."

"I've taken care of it."

"Your trust has taken care of it?"

She hadn't touched her trust. It was the only thing she had of her mother. "Scholarship," Gabby had told him.

"For what?" He'd sounded utterly shocked.

"Academics." Her face had flamed. Even now she recalled the searing heat. "I'm studying computer science."

"Mmm." He lifted the newspaper between them.

It wouldn't have killed him to congratulate her, to acknowledge that she had done well in getting a scholarship, or—what she'd hoped and prayed for—to show so much as a spark of interest that she was studying computer science, following in his footsteps.

But he hadn't. No reaction whatsoever. He'd given her nothing.

Gabby mentally shook herself. It didn't matter. She shoved the lid back onto the box and set it aside atop the dresser. None of it mattered. He didn't care. He never had. At least, he wasn't a hypocrite about it, pretending what he didn't feel. In an odd way, that helped. She had never expected anything, not even a modicum of kindness from him, and on that, he had never disappointed her.

She finished packing her room. The small floral box of childhood personal things, she placed near her handbag. The two filled boxes of non-personal items, she placed against the wall near the door.

In the hallway outside her father's room, she paused. Her heart beat fast and she steeled herself before walking inside. His room smelled like him. She glanced around and saw no personal items atop the dresser or chest on even on the night-stand. The absence of anything at all personal made the room look like him, too. She dragged in a jagged breath, felt the swelling of tears.

He might not have been eligible for Father of the Year by

anyone's standards, but he had been her father. She'd loved him, and she'd hated that he couldn't open his heart just enough to let her in. How different things could have been . . .

But they had not been different. He'd made that call. They both had lived with it. A tear slid to her cheek. She slapped at it and began filling boxes.

Finally, she finished the room proper and moved to the closet. She'd unloaded nearly all of it before she spotted a small green leather box. Curious, she lifted it and walked with it into the bedroom. Until now, this could have been any man's room. Nothing personal beyond his wallet, which purportedly had been stolen while he lay on the street waiting for someone to notice and call 911, and a laptop that looked brand new and untouched. Oddly, that personal-effect absence included his wedding band. He hadn't worn it, but considering he missed her mother enough to never speak her name, Gabby fully expected to run into it. Yet she hadn't.

She placed the green leather box on the corner of his dresser and opened it. It was stuffed with letters still in their unopened envelopes. Dozens and dozens of them. Gabby thumbed through them, checking the return addresses. All of them were from her Aunt Janelle.

Gabby's heart raced. She opened the first letter. *How many years will you keep Gabby from me? Why will you not let me see her or even speak to her on the phone? You're heartless, Adian. Spiteful and cruel. Are you still ignoring her? Acting as if she doesn't exist? I understand your hatred of me. I know too much and it terrifies you. But I will never understand how you can treat Helena's daughter this way. Never!*

Gabby stilled. Her jaw fell slack. Her Aunt Janelle hadn't forgotten her. She'd been forbidden from seeing or speaking to Gabby. Why? What too much did Janelle know? And why would her father hate her mother's sister for it?

Another realization slammed into Gabby. She hadn't been unlovable.

The knowledge washed over and through her. Janelle had loved her, and she had fought for Gabby. She'd failed, but oh what a difference it made to Gabby to know her aunt hadn't abandoned her. She had tried.

Gently, Gabby closed up the box and went down to the kitchen, eager to read the rest of the letters over lunch. Maybe in them she'd find out more. Maybe she'd learn something that could soften her heart toward her father. Because right now, she felt many things. Bitter and angry and confused. And she hated feeling any of those things.

At the kitchen bar with her sandwich and a bottle of flavored water, she began reading, and she read all of every letter. Before she knew it, she was done with them and with her sandwich. She learned nothing new except that her Aunt Janelle had suddenly stopped writing the year before Gabby graduated from high school.

After years of futile effort, she had finally given up. Gabby's vision blurred. She'd not given up easily, and there was a phone number. She had prayed that one day he or Gabby would use it. "If I'd known, I would have," Gabby whispered into the silent house.

It occurred to her she still could. She reached into her pocket for her phone and dialed the number.

Disconnected.

She tried searching, but there was no new listing. Her aunt had either moved or disconnected her landline. Either way, she wasn't where she had been. But if anyone could find her, Shadow Watcher could. Gabby texted him. "That offer of help still open?"

"You bet."

"I found some letters from an aunt I met once many years ago. She wanted to see me, but my father refused. I tried calling the number for her, but it's been disconnected. Would you see if you can find her? Her name is Janelle Reinhardt," she texted, then added the last known address. "I guess she never married, or she kept her name."

"On it," he said. "Be in touch."

"Packing. I'll message you when I get home tonight, if that's okay?"

"Anytime."

"Thanks, SW."

"Course, GK."

He'd find her. If Janelle could be found, Shadow Watcher would find her.

Her heart much lighter, Gabby taped a few boxes and headed back upstairs. The long hallway and its linen closet were all that was left to do upstairs. "Progress."

She emptied the closet in record time, then walked through each room to make sure she hadn't missed anything. When leaving her father's room and making a left into the hallway, she bumped her shoulder on a painting. The walls. She'd totally forgotten to empty the hallway walls.

When she lifted the third painting off its hanger, a panel in the wall slid open.

Surprised, Gabby lowered the painting to the floor, propped it against the wall, then looked inside the panel opening. A narrow frame between a couple two by fours made a shallow box. Inside it, on the raw wood, lay three thumb drives. Gabby's heart raced. This is what the killers had been looking for; these drives. Innately sure of it, she scooped them up and was halfway down the stairs before she recalled the killer had stolen her father's computer.

Grabbing her handbag, she headed to the office supply store, bought a dozen thumb drives and had four copies of each drive found duplicated. Not wanting to leave the store seemingly empty-handed—you never knew who was watching

—she picked up a couple spare rolls of tape and a roll of bubble wrap, which she needed to protect the paintings before boxing them.

Back at her father's, Gabby brought down the new laptop. As she suspected, he'd never used it. That struck her as odd, but worse, as unlikely for a man who would lose everything unless she put her neck on the line to help him. Maybe the killer hadn't missed seeing it. Maybe the killer had chosen not to steal it. Maybe the killer had left it, hoping she would use it and he'd see what she saw.

Lacking the equipment to ensure that wouldn't happen, she closed the laptop untouched, and returned to her apartment, where she tested a copy of the thumb drives.

Clean.

She opened the first one. Financial records. Spreadsheets with dates, names, and vast sums of money changing hands in all kinds of coded transactions. George Medros's transactions.

The other two thumb drives held the same kind of information and belonged to the same man. Gabby's heart thundered against her ribs. It didn't take a forensic accountant to see that Medros was violating at least a half dozen federal laws.

And her father not only knew it, he participated in it.

Why had he done this? Why?

One thing was clear. Medros or his henchmen would be back. With this kind of information out in the wild, they had to come back—and to keep coming back until they found the data.

And that explained why the FBI was involved in the murders. They wanted the data before Medros got it.

What was Gabby going to do to protect herself? She had to call Bain. If she didn't, she would be as legally vulnerable as her father. But if she did call him, and he went after Medros, the man would know Bain had gotten the data from her. Either way, odds were good she'd end up dead. Unless . . .

An idea struck her. She grabbed Bain's card, the three original drives and backup copies of each one, stuffed them all into her purse, and then left the apartment to return to her father's.

Using his house phone in the kitchen, she called the FBI agent's number.

He answered sounding irritated. "Bain."

"Agent Bain, this is Gabby Blake," she said, hoping she wasn't making the biggest, most deadly mistake of her life.

"Yes, Miss Blake?"

"I'm at my father's, emptying the house." She grabbed a fresh bottle of water from the fridge. "You asked me to call you if I found anything of interest."

"I did." He sounded engaged now.

"I found something of interest." She felt like a fool repeating herself, but if Medros or his people were watching her, she wanted to control what she let them see or hear. How they could not be watching her, she couldn't imagine. Not with all this detailed information about Medros's business loose.

"What did you find?"

"Well, I'm not sure exactly. Maybe something. Maybe nothing. Three thumb drives. I have no idea what's on them. The computer, you'll recall, was stolen."

"I'll be right over," Bain said. "Give me twenty minutes."

"That will be fine." She hung up the house phone. Her hands were shaking.

What had her father dragged her into? Why had he dragged her into anything at all?

CHAPTER SEVEN

Tuesday, December 8, 3:30 p.m.

WHEN THE DOORBELL RANG, Gabby looked through the peephole and saw a man she didn't recognize. He wasn't Bain. That much she knew for sure. This man was huge, older than Bain and in his fifties, she'd guess, bald with dark eyebrows and a salt-and-peppered mustache and beard, trimmed short and neat. His eyes were the coldest brown she'd ever seen in her life. And rather than the FBI suit and sunglasses Bain favored, this man wore a black shirt and a lumpy black jacket. Cold and wet, it clung to his chest. He was hiding something that printed in the fabric—a weapon.

Her heart slammed against her ribs and an instinctive warning sounded in her mind to not open the door. Her second thought was if she didn't open it, he'd shoot his way in. *Suck it up and stuff it down.* An idea struck her and took root. She plastered a smile on her face and opened the door. "Agent Bain?"

The stranger nodded. "His partner, Miss Blake." He looked oddly familiar, though she couldn't say why. Had she seen him before? If so, she didn't recall it. And why was he looking at her as if she'd risen from the grave?

She stepped back and let him in, praying she was doing the right thing. "It's good to finally meet you."

He seemed to relax and shielded his expression. "I apologize, Miss Blake, but I've been called with an emergency. Can I get the drives from you?"

"Of course." She retrieved them, covertly snapped a few photos of him, and then walked back to him and passed the drives over. "Like I told you on the phone, they might be something or nothing."

"You really didn't look to see what was on them?"

Gabby lifted her arms. "No way to look. The robbers took my father's computer," she said, amazed at the steadiness of her own voice. "To be honest, I wouldn't have looked anyway."

The skin between his brows puckered into two long creases. "Why not?"

"Apparently my father encrypted all his files. Even the household ones. His lawyer told me that opening them improperly will corrupt the data and it is imperative that a professional run them through special programs. That's the only way to be certain not to destroy them." She hiked a shoulder. "I have computer expertise, but I don't have those kinds of programs."

The man frowned. "That's a lot of trouble to protect a light bill."

She smiled. "It is. But you know how old-school people are. Set in their ways."

"I apologize for having to leave so quickly," he said. "I'm afraid there isn't any new information to report, and I really do have an emergency. They're waiting for me."

He didn't want to run into Agent Bain on his way out and be exposed as his fake partner. "No problem," she assured him, walking toward the front door. "I hope I haven't wasted your time, calling you over here about this. It could be nothing more than household items."

"Better safe than sorry." He stepped outside. "Thank you, Miss Blake." He turned back toward her. "Oh, one question."

"Sure." She wanted to shut the door and lock it but didn't dare to move.

"Was Rogan Gregos a client of your father's, or did he ever mention him?"

"I told you, I know nothing of my father's business."

"It could have been a personal relationship, from his childhood or something."

Rogan. It was an unusual name. Where had she heard it before? The answer danced just beyond the edge of her memory. "I'm embarrassed to say this, but the truth is my father didn't talk to me about anything. His childhood is as much a mystery to me as his business." She held the man's gaze, let him see the truth in her eyes. "Why do you ask?"

"An informant mentioned him once. Totally unrelated case." He turned away. "Thanks again for your call."

"You're welcome, Agent . . ." She waited, but he still didn't supply a name. Instead he rushed off the porch and down to his vehicle.

Gabby stood in the doorway until he stepped off the porch. *Rogan Gregos.* Who was he? And how did he connect to her father?

Having no answers, she put that aside to look into later, closed the door and locked it, then watched through the peephole until the man got into his SUV and pulled away. Her stomach in knots, she dropped to the floor, leaned back against the door and breathed deeply until she stopped seeing spots. He could have shot her. Might would have shot her if he'd thought for a second she knew he wasn't Bain's partner or if he hadn't believed that she hadn't seen the data.

She swept her hair back from her face with a trembling hand. She'd survived that round. Okay. Okay. Now what did she do about Bain?

4:00 p.m.

THE HOUSE PHONE had been tapped. Nothing else made sense. Even if Medros's henchman had been watching the house, the guy wouldn't have known to ask for the thumb drives or the need for speed in getting them and getting away before Bain arrived. The only way he could know that information was if he'd overheard both sides of the phone call from her to Bain.

Agent Bain arrived and, after they'd exchanged pleasantries and he'd informed her he had no new information on her father's case, he asked for the drives.

Gabby gave them to him. But instinct warned her to keep information about Medros's man's visit to herself, so she heeded the warning. The information belonged to Medros, after all, so it wasn't as if he didn't have the right to it.

"Have you looked at these?" Agent Bain asked.

Gabby could give him the same spiel she'd given Medros's man, but she didn't. Lying to the FBI was a lot different than deceiving a Medros thug, so she evaded, sidestepping. "They stole the computer, remember?"

"I do." He frowned. "So how do you know what's on them is of interest?"

"I don't, which is why I said maybe they're of interest. Or maybe they're not," she reminded him. "I have no means here to safely look at the drives."

A little confused, he cocked his head. "What made you think they might be of interest?"

She hiked an eyebrow. "Well, why else would my father hide them in a wall?"

"Fair point." His frown eased and he went on. "I understand you're an IT guru over at Handel."

"I work there in IT, yes."

"If my people need help deciphering the data, will you help them?"

Testing the waters to see if she'd be cooperative. There was little the FBI couldn't handle and even less that would require her help. "If I can, of course," she said. "But don't expect much. I know nothing about my father's work which means if I saw it, I wouldn't know what I was looking at."

"Understood." Bain rubbed at a graying temple, appearing more relaxed than he had been when he'd arrived. "We're hoping these drives contain information that will help us finally nail Medros."

Silence seemed wisest, not knowing if the phone or the house was bugged. So, she smiled and nodded.

Shortly thereafter, Agent Bain departed with a copy of the original thumb drives, no doubt eager to see for himself what was on them.

As soon as he looked, he would realize he had hit the Medros motherlode and be in a great mood. She almost envied him that. Almost. Because then he too would be a target.

She returned to her packing and second-guessed the wisdom of what she had done the rest of the afternoon. No matter what alternative she tried in her mind, she ended up vulnerable or dead.

By dark, nothing on that front had changed. Weary, she forced herself to keep working, eager to have this chore behind her and to drive away from this house for the last time. For the next few hours, she continued to spin scenarios, and finally concluded she'd done the best she could do to distance herself and convince both men she had no idea what she had given them. Nothing else afforded her more protection, and most alternate options offered her a lot less.

This was one time when ignorance was bliss.

Whether or not it was enough bliss to keep her alive remained to be seen.

Her phone rang. Recognizing Handel's ringtone, she answered, "Gabby Blake."

"Blake, it's Fitch. I hate to bother you, but I need help."

"With what?"

"We've had a security breach."

Handel didn't do security breaches. It stopped other businesses from having them. "I'll be right there."

Minutes later at the office, Gabby sat at her desk and began running diagnostics to assess the problem. Theirs was a complicated system and it took a good stretch of time, especially with Fitch standing over her shoulder, but finally she had her answers. "Handel hasn't been breached. I have," she told Fitch, then looked back at him. "Have you logged in on my computer?"

"No." He didn't meet her eyes. "Well, yeah, I did. I needed to run a backup and I didn't want to tie up my machine."

Gabby glared at him. "How did you get my password?"

His face red, he frowned at her. "You know how."

He'd hacked her. She let him see her fury. "Fitch, give me one reason I should not report you and recommend Peter Handel fire you right now."

Fear flashed through his eyes, settled on his face. "Blake. Gabby, don't. Please." He lifted a hand. "You don't understand. I had no choice."

"What do you mean?" She challenged him. "Of course, you had a choice."

Fear flooded his face. "This goon gave me until nightfall

to check out your computer and prove you hadn't uploaded anything from a thumb drive. He stood right here while I checked."

Medros's thug had dared to come here? She described the potential goon, Bain's fake partner and had-to-be Medros's man. "Bald, beard, fifties, black coat and shirt?" She didn't mention the weapon he carried.

Fitch's eyes lit up. "Yeah, that's him." Fitch frowned and dropped his voice. "He had a gun on me, Gabby. I had to do it."

She didn't doubt Fitch was telling the truth. He was far too scared to lie. "Did the goon give you his name?"

"No, but the identification he used to get in the building was for Rogan Gregos."

Surprise streaked up Gabby's spine. The same name he had asked her about at her father's house. "I don't know anyone with that name," she said, putting it out there. "What did you tell him?"

"The truth," Fitch said. "That you haven't been in the office since your dad died and there had been no remote access to your computer. It's not allowed. Corporate policy. And even if you tried, you'd be blocked by security protocols. Handel himself can't get around them."

That was why he'd taken the risk to come here. He had no other options. "Did he say why he wanted to know this information?"

"No."

A muscle twitched near his mouth. The one that said he wasn't being forthright. "Don't lie to me, Fitch."

"I swear. That's all of it. I looked at your computer and told him you hadn't accessed anything or uploaded anything. He took a photo of the screen with his phone, warned I'd better not be lying to him or he'd be back, and then he left."

That held the ring of truth. But there was something

more. She felt it down to the marrow of her bones. "What aren't you telling me?"

Fitch swallowed hard. "He said if I told anyone what he wanted in here he'd kill me." Fitch blinked hard. "He knew where my family lives, Blake. Where my kids go to school. He even knew I pick up my mom from chemo and that's why I'm late getting to work."

That surprised Gabby. She hadn't known that was the reason Fitch ran late. Guilt for her irritation with him about it set in. "I'm sorry about your mom." Why didn't Bain's fake partner who obviously worked for Medros just kill Fitch? She glanced up, saw the camera. He couldn't kill everyone in the building, and if he did, he still couldn't eliminate the video footage, which was stored on-site and in a remote location.

"Yeah," Fitch said. "This is her second round. So far, we're hopeful."

"I'll keep her in my prayers."

"Thank you."

Gabby didn't have to ask if he believed the man about the threats against him and his family. It showed in every line in his face. "How did he get into the building?"

"He said he was picking up a personal item for you. Convinced security downstairs that you needed something you'd left at the office. He had ID, of course." Fitch lifted his hands and let them drop to his sides. "I'm sorry, Blake. We all thought he was legit. He knew all about your dad and everything."

She nodded. "Okay. Write it up for the boss and I'll sign-off on it, too."

Fitch looked relieved. "Thanks, Blake."

"You were trying to help me."

"Who was that guy? What's he after?"

She checked her watch. Nearly midnight. "You don't want to know."

Her phone rang. She pulled it from her pocket and checked Caller ID. NOPD? "Gabby Blake."

"Miss Blake, this is Sergeant Falco, NOPD. Are you driving?"

"What?"

"If you are driving, could you pull over and stop, please?"

"I'm not driving. I'm in my office at work."

"Good." He paused. "Miss Blake, I understand that your father recently passed away. Was anyone living in his home?"

"No."

"Is anyone there this evening?"

"No. No one is there. Well, no one should be there."

"Any pets in the home?"

"No." What was going on? These weren't idle questions.

"So as far as you know, the house is empty then?"

How bizarre. "Yes."

"Good." Relief etched his voice. "Could you meet officers at the property as soon as possible then, please?"

"At my father's house? Why?" Her stomach knotted. "Sergeant Falco, what is this all about?"

"I'm sorry to have to tell you this, Miss Blake. "Your father's house just exploded."

CHAPTER EIGHT

Wednesday, December 9, 12:16 a.m.

THE ACTIVITY on her dad's street surprised Gabby. Fire
trucks lined up in front of his house—three of them, nose to
end—and a handful of police cars and emergency responders
stood parked on both sides, barricading the street. Gabby
pulled in behind the lot of them near the next-door neighbor's driveway and then exited her Mustang.

The acrid smell of soot and ash hung heavy in the air,
burning her nose. She stopped at the foot of the driveway
blocked by yellow crime-scene tape stretching around the
perimeter of the property, and just stared at what had once
been the house. Heaped rubble, bits and pieces of still
glowing embers, littered the ground. A short stone stack
likely part of the fireplace was the tallest structure to survive.
Even fairly distant trees were scorched and singed, leafless
and charred.

Agent Bain was speaking with Detective Marsh, the silver-
haired homicide investigator. Marsh turned to talk with a
uniformed officer, and she caught Agent Bain's eye. He

stepped over stretched water hoses spewing water and walked over to her. "Miss Blake."

"What happened?"

"The fire marshal hasn't made a determination yet but, from experience, it looks like an intentional explosion."

"But why?" She didn't get it. Why would they want to blow up the house now? She'd given them what they wanted.

Bain touched a hand to her arm and led her away from the cluster of people coming and going down the driveway. "Remember the confidential informant I mentioned to you earlier?"

She nodded.

"We heard from him again a short time ago. Actually, I was on the phone about him when I had the locals call you to meet me here."

The streetwise and connected confidential informant. "He knew this would happen before the explosion occurred?"

Bain nodded. "Warned us to get you out of the house."

"So, this was an intentional act." She absorbed the gravity of that. "Medros ordered it?"

Again, Agent Bain nodded. "He considers you a loose end. Medros doesn't tolerate loose ends."

"So he wants me dead?" She asked, but it wasn't a question really. Everyone in New Orleans who followed the news held strong suspicions of that about Medros. Witnesses disappearing, committing suicide, having fatal car accidents. That kind of thing can only happen so many times before it begins to stink to high heaven and points fingers.

Still Agent Bain answered her. "Yes, I'm sorry to say he does want you dead. Apparently, he's concerned your father had the thumb drives and additional backup copies of his information on the premises."

Or that she had backups. Gabby's stomach sank. No help for it. She was obligated to tell Agent Bain the whole truth now. "There were. I had copies made of the thumb drives I gave you. Before you came to the house to get them, another man showed up pretending to be your partner. I let him in."

"Pretending?"

She nodded. "Two had already been murdered in the house in the middle of the day. I didn't want to be the third victim, so it was safest for me to give him the lie and let him pretend." She paused and dragged in a settling breath. "I gave him the originals. They belong to him . . . Well, to his boss, after all."

"How do you know he wasn't my partner and he worked for Medros?"

"You'd have told me if your partner was coming instead of you. You didn't. And the suspect pool isn't that large. So far as I know, Medros is the only one in it."

"Fair points," Bain agreed. His expression relaxed. "Then what happened?"

"Then he left."

Bain's voice deepened. "Who was he?"

"I don't know. Like I said, he told me he was your partner. I gave him a couple of openings to tell me his name, but he never said it." She paused and thought back. "Well, he might have told me when he was on the porch, but if he did, the door muffled it and I didn't catch it."

"If you saw him again, would you recognize him?"

"Yes." She hiked her handbag strap on her shoulder.

"Did this man in any way threaten you?"

"No." Careful. Not too much. She couldn't risk getting Fitch or his family hurt by telling Bain that part. "He just took the thumb drives and left. He said he had an emergency. I suppose he didn't want to run into you, though that is total supposition."

"Likely a good one," Bain said. "If I show you a couple

photos of known Medros associates, will you see if you recognize the man?"

"Yes." Medros wanted her dead. How could she refuse to do anything that might hinder him and help keep her alive?

Agent Bain pulled out his phone. Detective Marsh joined them. "I'm sorry for your troubles, Miss Blake."

"Thank you." She nodded. Unlike Bain, there was a sincerity about Detective Marsh that appealed.

"The officers have been canvassing the neighbors," he said.

"Did anyone see anything?" she asked. Toward the house, a spray of sparks lifted in the wind.

"No one yet," the detective said. "Agent Bain has briefed me on events. Considering this," he waved a hand toward the now-collapsed house, "I think you should seriously consider entering a protection program."

Agent Bain frowned. "That's a little premature and extreme, Marsh."

He frowned at Bain. "For you maybe, but not for her. We both know we can't protect her. Not from him."

Him being Medros. Gabby's stomach fluttered. Bain was looking to make his case. Not to protect her. Marsh seemed to have her safety in mind, and he clearly didn't consider the police or the FBI able to provide for her safety.

Dipping his head, Marsh looked over at her. His silver hair caught the amber light from the streetlamp. "Where were you tonight?"

"Work. We had a security breach. I had to go in and help secure the system." And that was absolutely all she intended to say about it. Fitch's activities and the goon intrusion couldn't be shared. For her and Fitch, but also for Handel. A security provider being infiltrated? If that leaked—and it would—it could irreparably damage the company's reputation. She wouldn't have that on her shoulders as well. "Has anyone checked on Lucy's family, Detective Marsh?"

"We have. No incidents occurring there."

Further evidence Lucy was collateral damage, and this was all related to her father and now to Gabby. "Good." Finding something to be grateful for wasn't easy, but at least Lucy's family appeared to be safe, and Gabby was grateful for that, and that there wasn't more guilt heaping onto the considerable pile she'd already accumulated.

Agent Bain passed his phone. "Here are photos of a half dozen known Medros associates. Do any of them look like the man who came over here earlier today?"

Gabby paused to fix his image clearly in her mind. While she did, Bain told Marsh about the pretender and the thumb drives.

She reviewed the photos on Bain's phone. One through four, nothing. Five—Five was him. Her instincts alerted her to keep that information to herself. She hesitated, heeded them, and then flipped on to the sixth photo. "Sorry."

Bain's disappointment etched the lines in his face deeper and his jaw tightened. "Can you describe the man?"

Knowing they couldn't protect her and wanting to survive, she slightly changed her description. "Late forties maybe, over six feet, and a bad hairpiece—brown. His eyes were brown, too. His nose was wide, likely broken at some time, and his shoulders were really broad. He was a big man. Much bigger than my father. And fit."

"You're absolutely sure none of the photos I showed you are him?"

She hiked a shoulder, reluctant to dance around the truth again to avoid lying to him. Shadow Watcher would find out the man's identity. Him, she trusted more than anyone else, and he did have her protection uppermost in mind.

"That's it then." Detective Marsh stepped in. "You can go

home now, Miss Blake. We'll finish up here. Do consider witness protection. In your situation, it offers you the best odds for remaining safe."

"Thank you, Detective."

Bain interjected. "You'll have to testify, of course. If charges are brought based on the material on the drives."

"Testify to what?" she asked, then reminded him and informed Marsh. "I've never seen the information on the drives, and I know nothing about my father's business."

Bain blinked hard. "Chain of custody on the drives."

Bait, she thought. So Medros would think she knew more than she did, and she would lure him to Bain. "I see," she said. Her instinctive feelings that she had better protect herself, that Bain was out to make his case at her expense, were proven in that comment. Anger flared inside her. Gabby stuffed it down. "No problem," she said, watching Detective Marsh. He bit his lower lip but didn't say anything. "You can arrange that, correct?"

"We can and will," Bain assured her.

Marsh shot her a warning look.

"Great. I'll sleep on the witness protection thing and let you know what I decide tomorrow."

"No rush," Bain assured her.

Detective Marsh snagged her attention. "The media's arrived." His gaze swerved to a Channel 3 truck pulling up to the curb across the street. "Let me walk you to your car, Miss Blake. Guide you through the gaggle."

A cluster of people gathered on the sidewalk and street stood watching. Presuming they were neighbors, Gabby nodded. "Thank you." She fell into step at his side.

When they were out of Bain's earshot, Marsh dropped his voice to a whisper. "Don't do it."

She didn't glance his way. "Witness protection?"

"Testify." His gray hair curled at his ear. He swiped a hand over his mouth. "They'll kill you, and Bain knows it. Medros and his people are untouchable, Gabby. If there's a high place, he has friends in it. And I'm not talking about just New Orleans. Medros's interests stretch far and wide and really high."

"How high?"

"All the way high." Marsh shook his head. "Don't do it."

She'd drawn the same conclusion. "What should I do, Detective?"

Marsh paused at the door of her Mustang. "If you were my daughter, I'd tell you to vanish. Tonight. Just go." He looked around, then spoke softly. "These people don't stop coming, Gabby. They'll never stop coming. And they could be anyone."

Medros would likely hire an outsider. Someone distant and unconnected. Marsh's warning was sincere and offered out of concern for her. That touched her. "Thank you."

"Don't tell anyone where you're going. Don't contact anyone here once you've left. Ditch your phone, close your accounts—whatever you can do tonight—and start fresh far, far away."

"I could remind you that you're the police and you're supposed to protect me from criminals like these."

"If I could, I would. But I can't protect you against them. No one can. I told you, they're untouchable." His tone was frank and sober. "I'm being realistic and honest. Take it for what it's worth. I am trying to give you the best advice I've got for you to stay alive."

She measured the man and saw no conflict between his words and what was in his eyes. Marsh was doing his best. "Thank you, Detective Marsh." She meant it sincerely.

He nodded and opened her car door. "You're not safe at the apartment, either, Gabby. Actually, you're not safe so long as you're anywhere they'd expect you to be."

"I understand." In a rare moment of open honesty, she let him see the truth in her eyes. Relief washed through his, and she closed the door, mouthed a final silent "Thank you" and then followed his hand-signals to leave the tangle of cars and headed out of her father's neighborhood for the last time.

Two blocks away, she formulated a plan and checked her watch. Nearly two in the morning. Well, Shadow Watcher had offered to help, and he had said "anytime." She was in way over her head and smart enough to know it. She needed serious, competent help. In this minefield, serious, competent help she could trust.

She pulled over at an all-night grocery store and slid into a parking slot between two trucks, then grabbed her phone and texted Shadow Watcher.

In her crazy life, the irony of most trusting a man whose name she didn't know wasn't lost on her. But considering the majority of those who did know her name were out to kill her, contacting him didn't seem crazy at all. It seemed sensible and sane.

"Help. I need you." She sent the text.

His response was immediate. "What's wrong?"

"Complicated. Can I phone you?"

"Yes. Burner?"

Did she have a burner phone? She did not. She looked up at the all-night grocery store. "Fifteen minutes."

"Safe?"

"At the moment, I think so."

"Fifteen."

She bought a burner phone, returned to the car, then activated it and called Shadow Watcher. Her stomach was in knots. Male? Female? She had no idea what to expect.

"Hello."

Deep, husky voice. Definitely male. "It's me."

"What's going on?"

She quickly filled him in on events from Bain's visit to her apartment to Medros's man pretending to be Bain, then Bain getting the copies of the thumb drives. She relayed details of the breach at work by a man threatening Fitch, to her father's house exploding. Then she told Shadow Watcher about meeting Agent Bain and Detective Marsh at what had been her father's house, and what each of them had told her. When she'd relayed all she could remember, she added, "I was on my way back toward the apartment, to throw off anyone who might be following, but I can't go back there."

"Is anyone following you?"

"I haven't seen anyone, and I've been looking."

"Wise to stay away from the apartment," Shadow Watcher said. "Definitely shouldn't go back. I hate it that you can't collect personal items."

"It's just stuff," she said. "Well, except for a book of hand-made soap recipes that belonged to my grandmother. It's all I have of her."

"Nothing of your mother or father's?"

"No. Just the soap book." An empty ache crept through Gabby's chest. Silly, she supposed. She'd never met her grandmother, but she'd treasured that book. Long aspired to make every one of her soaps. Those she had made, she had loved. The lotions and oils, too.

Shadow Watcher paused, then changed the subject. "You realize, of course, Medros learned about the thumb drives way too fast."

"He did," she agreed. "I figure he tapped the house phone or bugged the house itself."

"Or Agent Bain told him." Shadow Watcher grunted. "Actually, my money is on Bain. He's all about making his case, and he indirectly contacted you about the explosion, too. Not Marsh."

"That's right."

"Odd. I can see a cop on the desk catching the call and phoning Marsh, but phoning the FBI? That should have taken longer."

"Bain said a CI contacted them. While on the phone about him, Bain had the local call me. A Sergeant Falco, if memory serves."

"So, Bain knew about the explosion before the locals did?"

"That's my understanding. The CI warned him to get me out of the house." She remembered the photos. "Bain also showed me some photos of known Medros associates. The man who pretended to be Bain was in them."

"Did you tell Bain that?"

"No, I didn't."

He sighed relief. "Give me a brief description. I'll dig and send my findings to see if we can peg him."

She reeled off a description of the man. "The guy who pretended to be Bain's partner, Medros's guy, asked me if I knew Rogan Gregos."

"Do you?"

"No, I don't," she said. "He wanted to know if Rogan Gregos had been one of my father's clients or if they'd had a childhood relationship."

"Did they?"

"I have no idea. I've never heard of him."

"But the questions got your attention."

"They did. He said the name had come up in an unrelated case and blew it off."

She was making too much of this. People got mistaken for other people or asked about people they didn't know all the time. It'd happened to her right before Thanksgiving. That old man with dementia had mistaken her for someone he knew named Helena. "Wait a second. Something just occurred to me. Medros's guy asking me about Rogan Gregos might not mean anything."

"Oh, I'm betting it means something."

"Sorry. I phrased that badly. When he went to Handel, he produced identification to Security that his name was Rogan Gregos," she explained. "It could be—"

"When he came to get the thumb drives, he dropped the name to you so when you heard it from Fitch, you'd know Medros's surrogate had come calling and to keep your mouth shut."

"Exactly," she said. "It was a warning." Something else niggled at her mind. She couldn't put her finger on it yet, but instinctively she knew she need to focus because whatever it was, it was important.

"That makes sense." Shadow Watcher sounded a little shellshocked. "And you're sure the name was Rogan Gregos?"

"Yes."

Shadow Watcher went silent for a long moment. "I'll check anyway and see what I can find. Meanwhile, I'm already convinced Bain's dirty." Shadow Watcher's tone left no doubt. He didn't like where this was going. "Has to be."

Her own reaction to Bain aligned with Shadow Watcher's. "I'm thinking Bain either told Medros straight out about the thumb drives or he somehow let him know. Otherwise, Medros's guy couldn't have gotten to me before Bain did. There was only a twenty-minute window."

"Bain well might have waited just out of sight until after Medros's henchman left," Shadow Watcher said. "Either way, Marsh is right. Bain's concern is his case, not your life, and Medros won't stop coming. We've got to get you out of there."

The wisdom in that conclusion tasted bitter. But she couldn't argue, the move was logically sound. "I agree."

"You have the drives with you?"

She frowned through the windshield, ran a visual

perimeter sweep around the car, and spotted nothing odd or strange. "How did you know I kept a copy?"

"You're the Gate Keeper. Of course, you kept a copy."

For a stranger, he knew her well. "They're with me."

"Hit the nearest ATM, withdraw all you can, and then head north," he said. "Use only this phone and contact only me. Don't email or text anyone. Don't call anyone else. Don't go anywhere anyone knows you. I'll get you what you need. Right now, just head north. When you're almost to Jackson, Mississippi, call me. That'll take about three hours. You up for that drive?"

Did she have any choice? "Yes." Honestly, she wondered if she'd ever sleep again.

"Okay, I'm going to alert the troops. We've got you, GK. Just head north—and don't get an hour or two down the road and re-think this. You're not making too much of it. You are in jeopardy. Bain learned too quickly about the house explosion, he heard too quickly from the CI there was a contract on your father and then on you. Medros found out too quickly about the thumb drives and had his goon intercept them. It's not that one thing is off, it's all off. Marsh might be clean, but his hands are tied. We don't know. But we can't bet your life on him keeping you safe when he's already told you he can't do it."

"I won't re-think it and turn around. I promise. But there's so much I'm leaving undone. My job—they're expecting me on Monday. My father's affairs. My apartment."

"Don't worry," Shadow Watcher said. "I told you, the troop is on alert. We'll handle everything. You just drive. Remember, call me before you hit Jackson."

Overwhelmed with emotion, Gabby swallowed hard. "Thank you, SW."

"Be careful and drive safe."

"I will." She ended the call reluctantly. What the troops

could do about the personal business she needed to handle she had no idea. But now wasn't the time to worry about any of it. He said they'd handle it, and they would handle it.

Dead women don't take care of anything.

Yet the world somehow limps on without them.

CHAPTER NINE

Near Jackson, Mississippi
Wednesday, December 9, 8:00 a.m.

GABBY STOPPED SOUTH OF JACKSON, Mississippi, to fill the tank with gas.

In the restroom, she soaped her hands then splashed her face with cold water and dabbed it dry. Afterward, she went into the convenience store and bought a large coffee. She wasn't at all sleepy. Fear put you on an adrenaline high like nothing else.

Back in the Mustang, she pulled away from the pump and over to the edge of the store's parking lot. The sun had been up for a good while and she'd watched cold wind whip at trees for miles. She texted Shadow Watcher from the burner phone. "Near Jackson."

"Call me."

Odd. But maybe not. She dialed his number.

"Hello."

"Good morning," Gabby said, then sipped at her coffee. Steam furled from the cup.

"You safe?"

"I think so." She was in the middle of nowhere.

"No one followed you or anything?"

"No." She'd checked her mirrors a thousand times. "I'm certain of it."

"Good." He let out a staggered breath. "TreasureSeeker tells me you hit three ATMs on your way out."

Not at all surprised by that, she admitted it. "I did. They were close by and I was there, so I thought I'd better seize the opportunity."

"Good thinking," he said. "Okay. I want you to drive on to Jackson then about six miles north of downtown. Off to your right, you'll see a tall sign for a Chevy dealership. Go there."

"Why?"

"You've got to change cars."

Change cars? Give up her Mustang? "But I love this car."

"No choice, GK. Unless you want to be in it when it's totaled."

"Totaled?" He couldn't be going to destroy her Mustang. After all she'd already given up, now this, too? Appalled, she tried and failed to keep a whine out of her voice. "But it's a vintage classic."

"It's necessary, Gabby. Troop Search and Rescue has evaluated the situation, and the only way you're going to survive this is if you're already dead."

She sputtered hot coffee. "What?"

He didn't repeat himself, just stayed silent and waited.

"Oh, God." Her mind went into overdrive. She grabbed a tissue and dabbed at the spewed coffee, swiped it off the steering wheel. "What about money? My job?"

"Consider everything gone." He sighed. "But don't panic. The troops are working on all of it. We'll do all we can to recover as much as we can."

How could they recover anything? "But—"

"Listen, either you trust us, or you don't," he interrupted. "Pick one now, because we're working hard to do this right. But if you're not on board . . ."

Trust. So hard. Relying on them, and their judgment. Her whole life was out of control. Apparently, her death, too. But did she have any choice?

She really didn't. She tossed the soaked tissue onto the floorboard. "Fine. I'm in."

"Okay, then. When you get to the dealership, a guy in a green shirt with red hair will walk up to your Mustang and pass you a key. He'll tell you where your new car is parked. Leave the Mustang, your purse and your old cellphone in it. Try to avoid anyone else. Get in the new car and then drive North. That's all you have to do."

"Okay." She could buy a new purse. A grocery bag would do until then. What did she think about this? It was all so alien to her that she couldn't even process it.

"Okay," he repeated. "Call me from Memphis. By then, I'll have more information for you."

More information would be good. Maybe she wouldn't feel like she'd been picked up and slung onto a different planet, one in an alternate universe. "Thank you."

He ended the call.

Gabby drove up the interstate and spotted the car dealership sign. Chevrolet. She took the exit, drove into the lot and then parked.

A man with red hair and a green shirt sauntered out of the building and over to her car. "Morning."

She rolled down the glass. "Good morning."

He passed her a set of keys. "Receipt, registration and proof of insurance are in the glove box, Ms. Johnson. Red Malibu, loaded, he pointed. Three cars down."

Ms. Johnson? "Thank you." She rolled up the window, gathered the money from her purse, left the credit cards and checkbook, dropped her phone onto the center console, and waited. The man walked back into the building. He didn't look like someone who would wreck a vintage car intentionally to make it look as if someone had died in it. Where would he get a corpse?

She didn't want to know. She *really* didn't want to know. There wouldn't be one, of course. How they'd pull that off, she had no idea. And she wanted no idea. Pushing further thoughts of the logistics from her mind, she left the keys in the ignition, and got out of the car.

Seeing no one, she walked over to the Malibu. It was a beautiful deep red with light and dark gray two-toned interior. Different. Far more modern than the classic Mustang, but once she got used to it, she could be okay with it.

Inside, she cranked the engine and gave her Mustang one last look. She'd loved that car. On top of everything else, she had to forfeit it, too. What was happening to her and her life wasn't fair or right but, long ago, she'd learned little in life is ever fair or right. It's just life. "Thanks for being there for me," she whispered to the Mustang, then drove out of the lot and got back on the Interstate.

By 1:00 in the afternoon, she reached Memphis, gassed up the car and grabbed a Chinese buffet lunch that seemed popular, gauging by the crowded parking lot. It was decorated for Christmas and an entire table of people all wore Santa hats. Their laughter grated at her raw nerves. Stuffed and suddenly sleepy, she made her way back to the lot and automatically looked for the Mustang. Catching herself, she remembered she drove a Malibu now and made her way to it. The cold chill pushed by a stiff wind cut through her.

By the time she opened the door, her teeth were chattering. The day was beyond chilly; it was cold. At least freezing, though she'd yet to see snow. She locked herself in and cranked up the heater. Stifling a yawn, she texted Shadow

Watcher. If he sent her much further, she was going to have to insist she stop for a nap. It'd taken fear, starvation and steel will to drive past the last rest area. She lacked the stamina to do it again.

"You holding up okay?" he asked.

"I'm tired now, but fine. Is wherever you're sending me much further?"

"Not much. I know it's hard but it's important you keep moving. Once you arrive, you'll be safe. Until then, you're vulnerable. Maybe even a target."

That zapped the sleep right out of her mind. "Where am I going to arrive?"

"Stay on I-55 for now, to St. Louis. Call from south of it for final instructions."

Final instructions. So, St. Louis wasn't her ultimate destination. "I might need a nap."

"If you do, you do. Be safe but try to keep pushing. It's important."

He knew something. He or someone in Troop Search and Rescue had picked up a warning or something. She should ask what, but she was too frazzled to deal with anything more. Her maximum tolerance level had been reached many miles ago. "If I have to stop, I'll let you know. Otherwise, I'll be in touch when I'm south of St. Louis."

"Great."

"You said you'd have more information for me."

"I do—but it'll have to wait. Incoming. Drive safely."

Gabby sighed and put her phone in the center console. Noticed that the car's control panel had a phone button. When she had time, she'd configure it. She left the parking lot and got back on the Interstate.

⚷

Near St. Louis, Missouri
1:30 p.m.

SIGNS FOR ST. Louis started appearing almost right away. About four hours away. That at least gave her an idea of about how long it would take her. Traffic was light, and for that she was grateful. She stopped just after three and got a large coffee, then headed out again.

At 5:30 she was just south of St. Louis. Rush-hour traffic was heavy, so she exited the interstate and pulled into a nearly empty school parking lot. From there, she texted Shadow Watcher.

"I'm here." She studied the sky. It looked dark and heavy, which fit with the radio's weather report predicting snow. She had no idea how to drive in snow, so of course, she'd have to deal with that, too.

"Any trouble?"

"None." She texted back. "Should there have been some?"

"It was possible. We set up a decoy. Doesn't matter. You're okay for now."

"I'm dead on my backside and need sleep." The heat wasn't helping. It was toasty warm in the car; the Malibu's heater worked great, but warmth added to her feeling sleepy. "What now?"

"About an hour to go."

"One?"

"One," he texted. "Take I-55 to I-70 East. You'll cross the Mississippi River into Illinois. Stay on I-70 until you see an exit for Christmas Cove. Take it, and at the Stop Sign at the foot of the clover, turn Right. Drive 7.2 miles. You'll see two mailboxes on the left side of the road. Turn in there and drive to the end of the road. There's a cottage. Inside, you'll find what you need."

"Do I need a key?"

"Second log on the stack."

The key was hidden in a log? Must be. "Okay. Thank you."

"Call and let me know you've arrived. It could snow before you get there. You ever driven in snow?"

Call not text. She made a mental note of it. "I've only seen snow a couple times in my life—including just snow flurries. No, I've never driven in it."

"Allow a lot of distance between cars, and don't slam on the brakes. You'll do fine."

He sounded confident. She didn't feel confident or even capable. "I'll call when I arrive." She stowed the phone, pulled back into traffic, and then started watching for the I-70 exit.

More irony. Whoever would have believed she'd land in a place called Christmas Cove, in Illinois? She who had never had a real Christmas in her life and had insisted she stop wishing for one years and years ago.

Christmas brought her father to mind and she couldn't help but wonder. Why had he insisted she stay with him if only to ignore her? Why hadn't he just sent her to live with her Aunt Janelle who clearly had wanted her? Life could have been so different for all of them. Instead he seemed to take some perverse pleasure in denying her aunt the right to even see or speak to Gabby and her, the security of growing up thinking anyone cared if she lived or died.

"Let go of it, Gabby. No time or energy for that. Not now." Grateful the weather was holding off, she spotted the turn-off for I-70, moved over a lane in front of an eighteen-wheeler truck, then took the exit and merged into traffic. Not much longer now, she told herself. "Suck it up and stuff it down, Gabby."

At 7:00, she spotted the Christmas Cove exit and moved into the right lane, took it, and drove the clover to its foot then braked for the stop sign. She followed Shadow Watcher's instructions and spotted a series of lakes with manicured lawns and tall, thick oaks. The largest weeping willow she had ever seen in her life hugged the road and draped nearly to the ground.

About the length of a ball field further she spotted two black mailboxes on sturdy wooden posts. She slowed, then turned onto the tree-lined road. On the right was a well-maintained farmhouse with a broad front porch and two swings, one on either end. She eased past the house on a narrow road that ran alongside it and kept going until the road stopped. A rustic cottage with a smaller porch and two rockers sat nestled under a canopy of trees.

"Charming." Gabby loved it. The flower beds needed some attention. Come spring, weeding and a few new plants would spruce them up, but the cottage itself, at least from the outside, appealed.

How long she'd be in this cottage or town, she had no idea. But for right now, she didn't doubt Shadow Watcher's saying she would be safe. The only way anyone could find this place is if they knew it was here.

She cut the engine and got out of the car, stiff and weary, longing for a shower and a bed.

CHAPTER TEN

The Cottage
Christmas Cove, Illinois
Wednesday, December 9, 7:35 p.m.

THE COTTAGE WAS pale-gray clapboard and trimmed in a darker gray. Low bushes planted near the windows were positioned so no one could hide behind them. The lawn was trimmed out with islands edged with stacked stones. Gabby stepped onto the porch and retrieved the key hidden in the bundled firewood, then opened the door and went inside.

Modern. Clean. Decorated sparingly in neutral, soothing tones. Very few personal items. Art, a blend that appealed to both men and women, and no photos littered the walls. She walked through to the kitchen. Spotless. Lots of light oak cabinetry and a long granite breakfast bar. Beyond it, a heavy oak table and four chairs. Stainless appliances. She opened the door of the fridge. Freshly stocked. So was the pantry, and stoneware dishes, pots and pans, and small appliances filled the cabinets. She closed the fridge door, wondering who had bought groceries and prepared the cottage.

In the living room, a big-screen TV above a stone fireplace stole the focal point. To the left stood a wet bar, and high above it, an oak railing and loft. French doors from the dining room and living room led outside to a broad covered deck that ran the length of the cottage with a huge grill and side-table on one end and, beyond a table for four, a porch swing on the other end. Flood lights penetrated the darkness and revealed lots of lush low bushes forming a hedge beyond the deck, and great shade trees with concrete benches near the trunks loomed across the lawn distant from the house. The landscaping was done with security in mind. Nothing encroached or gave anyone places to hide unless flat on their bellies in the dirt. A trail wound to some unseen place, and the quiet and calm settled around her.

Back inside, Gabby climbed the stairs. Exploring, she spotted two bedrooms, two baths, and the loft sitting area. In it, three walls were lined with books. She scanned the titles. An eclectic mix of fiction and nonfiction by familiar commercial and literary authors. The décor was warmer up here. The sofa plusher than the sleek off-white one downstairs. The owner clearly preferred sitting up here to read over watching TV downstairs. She liked it better, too.

Walking on, she entered the master bedroom. The bed took up the lion's share of the room. Appealing with its warm beige silk bedspread and drapes that matched the throw pillows on the king-size bed. Peeking through the window, she saw wooden shutters. Opening them, a beautiful view of the landscaped yard and, past it, woods with that wide trail. It led to a gazebo with two swings and bench seating. Beyond it was a little strip of beach and a body of water. Was that Christmas Cove? *Pretty*. She closed the shutters, and let the drapes fall back into place.

The wrought-iron and heavy wood furniture were definitely masculine, but delicate and intricate carved details in the wood softened the hard lines. She would be comfortable here, she thought, then walked on into the adjoining bath.

"Be still my heart." A spa tub. A big one. And a glass-walled shower. It was a huge bath and closet. Unable to resist, Gabby turned the water on in the tub, let it begin to fill, and then moved to the closet, hoping it wasn't empty and there'd be something in it she could wear.

Clothes hung there. A man's clothes. Extra Large. Big and tall labels. Had to be at least 6'2 to wear those. She moved from the hangers to the shelves, snagged a blue T-shirt and a pair of plaid pajama pants. Could they be Shadow Watcher's? That they might be his somehow comforted her, made her feel a little less alone. At the far end of the closet, she noticed a small washer and dryer stack.

"It's perfect." Who this place belonged to might be a mystery, but no one could fault his taste. She'd expected rough and rustic. But she'd found the whole cottage warm and welcoming, comfortable and cozy, and it had an understated elegance she hadn't expected to find in any wooded cottage, especially one in the middle of nowhere.

Back in the bath she grabbed a towel, eager to wash away the road grime, call Shadow Watcher and report her arrival, and then crash in the bed she hoped would be as comfortable as it looked.

How she slept tonight wouldn't tell her a thing. She was so exhausted she could sleep standing up. Tomorrow night would be the big test.

Half an hour later, dressed in the T-shirt and pajama bottoms, she crawled into bed and dialed Shadow Watcher on the burner phone.

"Where have you been?" He sounded hyper-alert and anxious. "You should have arrived there nearly an hour ago."

"I'm here, and I did." She should have phoned him first.

His worry pulsed through the phone to her carrying serious guilt. "Sorry." She said and meant it. "I took a bath."

"Oh." He paused. "But you're okay, right?"

"I'm fine." She swallowed hard. "Thank you."

"Thank God." His relieved sigh cracked static through the phone.

He had been seriously worried about her. Her guilt doubled. "I really am sorry I didn't call right away." She punched the pillow, settled in. "I—I'm not used to thinking about things like that."

"Like what?"

"Causing worry." She dropped her voice, more than a little uncomfortable. But he deserved an explanation even if it embarrassed her. "It's new to me."

"Surely your father—"

"No." Other kids had to report in, had curfews, phoned home when they'd be late. Her father kept her firmly on ignore and likely didn't notice when she was there or not.

"That explains a lot."

Having no idea what to say, she remained silent.

"Are you finding everything okay at the cottage?"

"Yes. It's great." She turned onto her side and grunted. "Whose clothes am I wearing?"

"The owner's," he answered cryptically. "Sorry, I didn't think about clothes."

"Does he always keep the fridge stocked?"

"Not always." Shadow Watcher paused again, as if wrestling with what to say and what to hold back. "You have a package incoming. Watch for it tomorrow."

"Okay."

"Two packages actually."

"What are they?" She swept her hair back from her face.

"You'll see. Nothing exciting, but definitely essential."

"Mysterious."

"A little." He dropped his voice. "Until you get both, stay put in the cottage."

His uneasiness settled into her. She'd picked up on this tone before, when something had gone south on a child-finding mission. "Have we hit a snag on something?"

"Everything is all right. You just need a few essentials before interacting with anyone. Lay low until then, okay?"

"Okay." Tilting the receiver away from her mouth, she yawned. "Thank you again for everything."

"Not necessary. Just call me when the packages arrive and keep your promise."

She'd promised not to get a few hours into the escape and turn around. Obviously, she had kept it. Had she made another promise and forgotten it? Possible, considering. "What promise exactly?"

"Stay alive."

"I'll do my best," she said, and meant it, too. "In case I haven't mentioned it, you're awesome. Doing all this for me . . . Honestly, I'm overwhelmed."

"Remember you said that." He sounded serious and yet a lightness in his tone laced his words with humor she didn't get.

"I will never forget. That, I can promise you." No one ever had done for her what he had. Ever. "Night."

"Good night, GK. Sleep tight."

Thoughtful, she placed the phone on the nightstand and turned off the lamp. Now why would he caution her to remember his kindnesses?

Before she could answer that question—nearly before the question had fully formed in her mind, she fell asleep.

CHAPTER ELEVEN

Thursday, December 10, 7:30 a.m.

THE FIRST PACKAGE arrived just as Gabby sat down to eat breakfast. It was a large white envelope, and she didn't have to sign for it, which pleased her immensely since she had no idea what to claim as her name. Had he stuck with Johnson, or changed it again?

A UPS guy in uniform dropped the package right outside the front door and rang the bell. He didn't wait for a response.

When he climbed back into his delivery truck and headed back down the driveway then drove out of sight, Gabby retrieved the package and took it back to the breakfast bar in the kitchen.

She forked a cluster of scrambled eggs into her mouth, then reached for the envelope and opened it. Small items tumbled out: an Illinois driver's license, a credit card, a new phone, and a wad of cash. She counted it. A thousand dollars.

No note. Not a word, and she'd bet not a fingerprint.

Gabriella Johnson. So that was to be her new name. Too

formal a name for her choosing, but it was pretty and at least she had a name again. And, a great personal perk. She could still go by Gabby. Odd, how much better that made her feel. When you've lost everything, anything familiar helps loosen the knots in your stomach about being so isolated. For most of her life, she had thought she couldn't be more isolated than she'd always been, but she had been wrong. Then she'd had her identity. Now even that was gone. The feeling of floating alone on the planet untethered and without anyone to even notify if she really died . . . that was the epitome of isolation.

The ID, money and credit card mocked her thoughts.

People floating alone didn't get envelopes like this. She tapped a fingertip to the stack of money and credit card. Where had Shadow Watcher gotten this money and card?

Heat surged up her neck to her face. She hoped the troops hadn't had to take up a collection for her. That would be awful, especially considering all the work they'd already been doing on her behalf. Did she dare to dream they'd somehow gotten into her accounts and transferred her money to some obscure account she would be able to access? Afraid to even wish for that, instead she settled on being grateful for what she held in her hands. Some cash and a new identity. By the grace of God, she hadn't been stopped between Jackson, Mississippi, and her arrival in Christmas Cove. Thinking about what would have happened had she been pulled over for anything put all those knots right back in her stomach.

Dead women don't drive.

She finished her eggs, then phoned Shadow Watcher, hoping she didn't wake him after keeping him up all night during her travels.

"Good morning."

"Morning," she said. "Sleep well?"

"Definitely. You get the packages?"

"One of them." She took a sip of hot coffee, watched the

steam lift from the cup and coil in the air. "Where did all this come from?"

"Don't worry, you're legal."

Impossible. "How?"

"We couldn't trust Agent Bain, but I have an FBI contact who is trustworthy. He's arranged things for you on the QT. Justin Wade is his name. You'll find his mobile written inside the envelope."

She looked and saw the phone number written inside. "Okay. So, he provided the driver's license and credit card?"

"And the cash."

Not Shadow Watcher or the troops, but Justin Wade, an FBI friend of Shadow Watcher's. No way was she going back to New Orleans to testify to anything. The vivid images of her father and Lucy that repeatedly popped into her mind warned her she'd end up just like them. "In exchange for what?"

"He knows what you're up against and doesn't want to watch you die—again."

Her breath hitched in her chest. She swallowed a lump that lodged in her throat. "So, I'm already dead?" The Mustang was wrecked, and she was dead. That's what Shadow Watcher was telling her, wasn't it?

"Just after dawn this morning."

Thursday, December 10th. Gabby Blake died at dawn. A chill swam through her body. She rubbed at her arm, seeking comfort. "Where?"

"Florida," he said.

How had they gotten the Mustang to Florida? She halted the question before she asked. She really didn't want to know. Ignorance wasn't just bliss, it was protection for her and for Shadow Watcher, the troops and whoever else they recruited to assist them.

"You ran off the road and down a steep embankment, clipped a massive pine and ended up in a shallow creek."

Her breath staggered.

"Disconcerted?"

"Well, yes," she admitted. "Honestly, I am."

"I know this part is hard, and I'm sorry. But considering Medros is involved . . . Well, dead is your best defense. For what it's worth, the troop vote was unanimous, and Justin agreed."

Medros had a long reach. "It's a good call," she admitted. If she had been voting, she'd have voted with them herself. "I just have to get used to it." That was a remarkable under-statement.

"Logically, it's the best option. Emotionally, it will take a little time."

"Yeah. I'm discovering that already." She sighed. "So, what happens now?"

"Now, you build a life."

It sounded so easy. So liberating. But how did she go about it, especially without resources? Thinking of all the money and assets she'd left behind soured her stomach. "I need a plan."

"For once, do something radical."

"Radical?" Wasn't what she'd just done radical enough? To her, she'd had a bellyful of radical.

"Plan a life you really want," he said. "It's your turn now. Grab this chance with both hands."

She thumbed the edge of the envelope, sipped at her tangy orange juice. "That's a whole new mindset for me."

"It is," he said. "That can be a bit overwhelming. Having so many choices to make on so many things."

"A bit." Actually, she was drowning in decisions that had to be made, and she likely hadn't yet thought of all the questions.

"May I make a suggestion?"

"Please." She tilted the phone, wiped at the counter with a dishcloth. "I'm sort of reeling."

"Anyone would be."

No judgment. No ridicule. And no pity. Just the facts. That made her feel a lot better. Calmer. "What's your suggestion?"

"Ditch all rules except one."

She paused, leaned a hip against the cabinet. "Which one?"

"This is your life. Only include things in it that you love. Forget everything else."

She dragged her teeth over her bottom lip. Impractical, but exciting. "That is radical."

"Yes, and it's also overdue. It's time to have a little faith in yourself, Gabby. You'll settle into it, too."

She hoped he was right. Boy, did she hope it. "I think it's going to take a while to get over the fear of being found."

"Why? No one looks for a dead woman."

"They don't if they know the woman is dead."

"Oh, they'll know. Troops are seeing to that. Actually, Agent Bain will be finding out in about half an hour. We notified the good detective who warned you to run—he'll get the word out."

Detective Marsh. "He'll suspect I followed his advice to vanish."

"If he acts on that in any way, we'll know it. Then we'll know which side he's on, too." Shadow Watcher's voice dropped, hardened. "Medros will be informed before the morning is out."

So that would end it. They'd run checks to see if she'd communicated with anyone in Florida—she hadn't—the case would go cold, and that would be that. Gabby Blake would be dead and gone and forgotten.

Her life being so effortlessly erased both elated and bothered her. It should be hard to wipe out a life, shouldn't it? Granted, it hadn't been much of a life—her work at Handel, with Troop Search and Rescue, her semi-annual visits with her father—but it had been her life. After a few moments of shock at Handel, she really would be forgotten. It was pathetic really. The person who would most miss her would be Fitch. She wouldn't be there to cover for him at work when he ran late.

"I wouldn't waste time being worried about anyone coming after you. You're protected."

He, the troops and Justin Wade had seen to that. They'd had her back. And here she worried about a life she hadn't been crazy about while living it. She shuddered. Realigned her thoughts. No more fear of being followed or watched. And no more emptiness, meaningless life. She wanted better. More. She wanted to matter to someone. "Thank you, SW. And thank Troop Search and Rescue for everything. I expect all this has had them in a whirlwind."

"It has been busy. But every single one knows if the shoe were on their foot, you'd be right there for them."

She would. And that they knew it made her feel a lot better about her old life. "I don't know how I would have managed alone. Obviously, I couldn't have—"

"You're not alone. Those days are gone. Never again will you be alone, Gabby. That's a promise. Got it?"

Her eyes stung. Such a good man. She smiled. "I'm seeing a shiny halo above your head."

He laughed. "Hardly."

The sound warmed her, and she actually smiled. "Whose home is this—in case someone asks?"

"Just say Plumber's cottage. Everyone in the cove knows Plumber, and no one uses addresses there."

"Does he live in the farmhouse?"

"When he's in town."

"Is he in town now? I should speak to him about how long it's convenient for me to be here."

"Not at the moment, no. But you're welcome to stay in the cottage indefinitely. Already arranged that. The cove is a friendly place, so long as you're not anti-Christmas. They love Christmas there."

"I love it, too," she confessed. She'd made ornaments, put up the scraggly tree no one else wanted, listened to Christmas music, and started her own tradition of attending a different church service every Christmas morning then bingeing on Christmas movies. "I have zero experience celebrating it with other people, but it's a wonderful—"

"Well, you're in the right place to celebrate it now. Look forward, not back. Oh, and you can trust Plumber. He's away at the moment, but his sister is there."

"Can I trust her, too?"

"Yes and no."

"Not tracking, SW."

"Yes, she's a good person, and if you need anything, you can contact her. Kelly Meyer. Her info is taped to the inside of the cabinet door near the fridge. But, no, she doesn't know your story."

"Okay." That thought was comforting. She had someone here and someone who would be here. "Why Johnson?" She wasn't opposed to the name, but she was curious. Was there significance in it?

"Why not?"

"No reason. I just wondered." So, was it his name, or Plumber's real name? Or one picked out of thin air?

"Justin had an emergency package put together. He kept Gabby because you shouldn't have to lose that, too. Not after giving up everything else through no fault of your own."

"That was thoughtful of him."

111

"I might be crossing a line here, but I'm going to do it anyway."

She stiffened, bracing for whatever came. "Go ahead."

"Take a few days to think about the life you want to build, Gabby. Stay off the Troop Search and Rescue chat, off all your Internet media sites—that includes that familysecrets.life you often visit and sometimes quote—and don't contact anyone on anything to do with your old life. More is inbound. Wait a couple days before venturing out. Until you get a better grip on your new circumstances."

"Okay." She hadn't taken a couple days to just do nothing in a long time. Of course, she wasn't going to do nothing now. She'd stay sequestered at the cottage, but she'd be planning a life. Her life.

Maybe the most important work she'd ever done. And, she prayed, it would be the most successful.

"Behind the cottage there's a path to a dock. From it, you can see the cove. Toss the old phone there. Remove the battery and then do that right away."

"As soon as we're done here." She went on, asked him the question she'd awakened with on her mind. "Are you this good to everyone?"

"I wish I could say, yes, of course, I am. But the truth is, no, I'm not."

"Why me?" she blurted out before checking herself. "Because I'm one of the troops?"

"Because you're you." He ended the call.

Gabby's jaw went slack. What was she supposed to think of that? For a long minute, she just stared at the phone totally perplexed. Being protected and treated so well because she was herself was outside her realm of experience. She had no experience, nothing to grasp, for a clue of his intent.

Fortunately, she'd been spared from responding. Grateful for the reprieve, she grabbed her coat and shrugged it on, snagged the old phone and removed the battery, then headed out the French door. She crossed the deck, then the lawn and walked down the trail to the water's edge.

Standing at the edge of the gazebo, she looked out on the sparkling sun-drenched water. She'd died today. Died, and her Mustang was gone forever. Her old life was gone forever. Her emotions rioted. Rebelled. She locked her knees to stay upright, stared out at the ripples the wind lifted on the water's surface, and slowed her breathing to calm herself. The sharp wind stirred the trees lining the bank and cast dancing shadows on the dappled ground and the water's edge.

Her hand throbbed. She lowered her gaze and realized she was squeezing the phone with all her might. The crisp morning air had a bite to it. Refreshing, yet inside an icy chill pulsed through her. Why was tossing a stupid burner phone into the water proving even more difficult than abandoning her beloved Mustang?

A knowing seeped into her. It wasn't the phone. It was accepting her own death. And letting go of her old life.

Resentment ignited in her. She hadn't been done with that life yet. It might not have been a perfect life. Honestly, there wasn't much in it she had liked much less loved. But it had been *her* life, and she'd worked hard, really hard, to build it.

For all the wrong reasons.

Shadow Watcher had been right about that. She'd chosen a career she didn't love to please a father who despised her and wasn't at all hesitant to keep her on a shelf away from him until he needed to put her into lethal jeopardy to bail him out of trouble for poor decisions he made in his choice of business associates. He'd waited too long to snatch her from that shelf. She'd failed. He'd died. Taken Lucy with him and shredded Gabby's last hope of ever having any kind of a relationship or bond with him. So, aside from her grandmother's soap recipes and her considerable savings, what exactly was Gabby leaving behind?

There weren't any warm and fuzzy memories. There were tons of memories of staying quiet and out of the way. Of being ashamed of being unlovable and unwanted. Of trying to fade into the background and escape anyone's notice. Of avoiding entanglements with others because she couldn't bear for them to know her sole parent considered her worthless and she had no reason to feel differently herself. That had been hard. Merciless. But even more merciless had been memories of year upon year of incredible loneliness. No real friends. Friends asked questions, made comparisons and judgments. But there was one thing she'd miss. The one thing she'd done for herself.

Engaging with Troop Search and Rescue. There, with that group of strangers, she'd been accepted, respected and even valued. Anonymous, yes, but that too now was gone. So, what in her old life was left to miss?

Nothing.

That cold fact slapped her hard. Her eyes blurred, and she blinked fast, dredging deep for resolve and determination, relieved when both swelled inside her. She had a second chance here. An opportunity for a fresh start that most people never got. Her new life could be whatever she wanted it to be with a few limitations. She couldn't return to New Orleans or to Troop Search and Rescue, or to a job like her old one. But the forced job change was a blessing not a curse. And, at least for a while, she had to keep an eye out for Medros's men.

Yeah, people didn't look for dead women, until they did. She'd keep her guard up, just to stay on the safe side. There was only one thing worse than losing a life you didn't love. Losing one you did. She had no intention of letting that happen.

As limitations went, hers weren't bad. She could do this. "You want better? You want more? Then do better for yourself this time."

She drew back her arm and hurled the phone into the water. "Goodbye Gabby Blake."

CHAPTER TWELVE

Thursday, December 10, 9:15 a.m.

WHEN GABBY RETURNED to the cottage, the expected second package lay waiting on the front porch outside the front door.

A box, this time.

Her fingers nearly frozen, she lifted the cardboard box and carried it through to the breakfast bar. She hunted down a pair of scissors, found them in a kitchen drawer, and then sliced through the tape and opened the box.

"A computer?" Shock fell to excitement.

A laptop—and a typed note taped to its top. "Don't call me except in case of an emergency. Go to protonmail.com. Account in your name. Password—don't change it—is *Anonymous-Season*. Don't "send" anything on this account. Saved draft emails only. This account is solely for us to correspond. Create a second account through a different carrier for all other correspondence. Do not search for or contact anyone you used to know. Do not access any old accounts of any kind. I'll be in touch when I can. A couple days. SW says you know the drill. Heed it. And stay alive."

It was signed, "J."

Justin Wade. So, he knew where she was, and he'd sent her a computer? Why?

She went to protonmail.com and checked. There was a draft email from "J" waiting for her. "Okay, so we deal in drafts but don't send emails. Got it," she whispered, and clicked to open the draft.

"No names. No sends on this account. Anything odd shows up, call the number provided. Otherwise, drafts only, this account only. Extra security precautions have been taken. Check this account tomorrow for the latest information. After then, unless something comes up, I will check in on Saturdays. Expect two deliveries tomorrow. Two items. One draft here, one package by truck. You don't know me, and I have never heard of you."

The truth slammed into Gabby. Justin Wade was helping her off-the-grid. Which meant he had no protection and neither did she. It also meant, like Shadow Watcher, Justin didn't trust Agent Bain. Or someone in his own organization. Maybe both.

That should worry her, but it didn't. It confirmed her judgment on Bain had been valid. A judgment mirrored by Shadow Watcher and confirmed by Justin Wade. Those affirmations of her instincts were reassuring. Their combined skills were far more honed.

A second draft came through. She confirmed the sender, then switched to read it.

"All drafts are military-grade encrypted and will be corrupted once opened and closed. Commit to memory. Don't print or preserve a copy in any way, shape or form."

The first draft she had read, she noted, had disappeared.

So even if NSA or the server preserved a copy, it would

preserve a corrupted copy. It was imperfect, but the best shot they had for retaining privacy. Which was to say, unless someone looked really close, dedicated time and resources, they wouldn't find anything.

She went through the software programs. The laptop was loaded. Justin must have owed Shadow Watcher huge to send her this. How in the world would she ever repay him—either of them—for all they were doing for her?

No documents on the laptop or in the envelope. She double-checked it. No letter and no note. Just licenses, including the Malibu's title and registration, all registered in her new name with the cottage's address. And all backdated to before Gabby Blake's father's attack, much less his death and her own.

Thinking about that rattled her. She sucked in a couple of deep breaths, pushed away the reality that she was homeless, jobless, and nearly broke, and poured herself another cup of coffee. She was alive, and that was a big something, considering. She needed to suck it up and look ahead. Period. Full stop.

Her mind a little clearer, she sat back down at the breakfast bar to plan her life. "Okay, Gabby Johnson." She set the mug beside the laptop atop the breakfast bar. "This is it—your second chance. What do you want most?"

FAMILYSECRETS.LIFE

WWW.FAMILYSECRETS.LIFE

THE TRUTH ABOUT RUNNING FROM DEATH

Running from truth is like running from death.
Eventually, it's going to catch you.
When it does, you'll discover that running from death
is inextricably twined with running from life.
It's impossible to run from one
without running from the other.
And like secrets suddenly revealed,
that discovery can be merciful or merciless.

— FAMILYSECRETS.LIFE

CHAPTER THIRTEEN

Thursday, December 10, 6:45 p.m.

WHO KNEW?

Gabby had stared at the blank screen for hours. Lunch had come and gone, the afternoon had come and gone, and still the laptop's screen remained totally blank. Figuring out what to do with your life when you could choose anything was a huge challenge. Having too many options was just as bad as having too few options. Where did you start? Geographically? Where did she want to live? What skills could she claim, computer security aside? That had to remain off the table, of course. She glanced at the clock on the microwave above the stove. Dinner time, and here she sat still groping for the right starting point.

Frustrated, her elbow propped beside the laptop on the breakfast bar, she sank her bent head into her hand and squeezed her eyes shut. When she opened them again, the blank screen mocked her. This should be easy. It should be a dream come true, to actually get to pick and choose the things you love and want in your life and ditch everything you don't want. So why was it so hard?

Having no answer, she scuffled to the fridge and pulled out the makings for a turkey and Swiss sandwich. Foraging in the pantry, she found a bag of chips. "Maybe you're going about this all wrong," she told herself. "You have no experience thinking about what you love or want." That was sad but true. She'd spent her life trying to please her father. To get his attention and win his affection. She'd failed, but she had remained determined. She'd structured and spent all her mental resources on winning him over.

Now, everything had changed. She had to shift her thinking. But long-time habits are hardest to break, right? So how did she make that mental shift?

She thought about it halfway through the sandwich, and finally a method occurred to her that might work. It was worth a shot. "Maybe you should start with what you don't want."

Biting down on a chip, she slowly chewed, casting the laptop screen a sidelong look. What a person doesn't want is important. Maybe it's every bit as important as what a person does want—and she definitely had more experience with that. It was in her comfort zone. As she polished off the turkey sandwich, ideas began floating through her mind.

She didn't want a desk job from 9 to 5 working for someone else. Translated, she wanted to be her own boss. She entered that on the page. "Okay," she said aloud. "Where?"

It didn't much matter. She'd only ever lived in New Orleans and she could never return there. A small town sounded a lot more appealing than a large one. Maybe a place with a sense of community. She had no family, but it'd be nice to one day have friends. At least, to feel accepted and as if she belonged.

That was important to her, but in this grand scheme of things, it had to be a lower-level decision that didn't need to be made now. What she would do to earn a living held far more urgency, and to an extent, it could govern where she chose to live.

A thought took hold in her mind and ignited a fire in her bones. If she had her grandmother's recipe book, she'd make soaps. Peppermint and oatmeal and aloe and lemon. She'd love that. Probably not much of a market for them, but how much of a market did she need?

"Dream, Gabby," she told herself. Her whole life, she'd done the smart thing, taken the surest steps, the least risks. "Yeah, you did," she muttered to herself. "And look how that turned out for you." She had lost everything. *Consider it gone,* Shadow Watcher had said. Her mother's trust fund that she'd never touched because it was all she had of her. Her considerable savings and investments. Her home and all she'd put into it. Her beloved Mustang. Her life . . .

She bit into a crunchy, salted chip. Maybe once you lost everything, the idea of losing everything isn't as scary. Either way, she added to her list. "Make soaps." In her mind, she smelled the oatmeal pomegranate, the lavender and cucumber and the peppermint. She'd loved the peppermint. It had been marked with a heart in her grandmother's book. She'd added a heart of her own. "Supply local stores? Open an online shop? One day, have a store of my own."

Now she was cranking. This approach worked much better. What else did she not want?

Before she realized what exactly she was keying, she watched the words appear on the screen. "Never spend another Christmas alone."

A hard lump stuck in her throat, and her breath hitched in her chest. Odds on that not happening didn't look good.

The old Gabby would have accepted that and moved on. The new Gabby didn't. She could fix it. She wasn't sure how, but she had fifteen days to figure it out. If she did, great. If not, then by next Christmas, she would be celebrating with a group. Some group of some kind. Somewhere.

In bold type, in all caps, she made Gabby Johnson's first promise to herself:

NEVER AGAIN WILL I SPEND CHRISTMAS ALONE

Satisfied for now, she saved the document and turned off the laptop. The progress had been slow, tedious, and more painful than she could have expected in ways, but it had been constructive. Gabby Johnson wasn't floating in the ether without a tether or anchor or even a clue anymore. Seeds of her future had been found. Now she just had to plant them, water them, and see what grew.

Why, she asked herself, had she never thought to do this before now? To really think about what she wanted and didn't want in her own life? What she loved?

The answer was complex and jumbled into feelings of wanting to belong, to be family and not blood strangers. It went to spending a lifetime being an unwanted nuisance. To being unlovable. Oh, Aunt Janelle might have fought for her, but did she want Gabby or just to win the battle against Gabby's father? More likely the latter, since her aunt didn't know Gabby. One meeting did not create bonds. They too were blood strangers. That truth stung, but better to face even hard truths than to live with comforting lies. There'd be plenty of those in her future, which was regrettable but essential to her staying alive. Yet she could not deliberately add more lies to the essential ones. That was a thin line she must never cross. Couldn't cross and still meet her own eyes in the mirror. Self-respect demanded it.

Yawning, Gabby called it a night. She locked up and then headed upstairs. The stress and adrenaline high had ended and now it was all she could do to make it up the stairs.

By the time she got into bed and settled in, she was half-dozing, but still her mind wouldn't shut down. The cottage was silent in a way her apartment or her father's home in New Orleans never had been. Memories started running through her mind. Unpleasant memories. Chilling images of him and Lucy on that office floor.

Gabby flopped onto her side and punched her pillow. "Not going there. Not tonight." Forcing her mind elsewhere, she focused on something good. A week ago, she had a different life. She had Troop Search and Rescue and no one else. Now they were not in her life, but she did have not one but two men she trusted—and that was a first. Shadow Watcher and Justin Wade. And once she met him, she'd have a third. Plumber. Shadow Watcher said she could trust him and his sister, Kelly Meyer.

Wasn't it a kick that she had absolutely no idea what any of them even looked like? That she only knew two of them by actual name? That she could walk right past any or all of them on any street in world and never know it?

There was something appalling about that.

Shadow Watcher had told her to stay put for a few days and not to venture into Christmas Cove. But as soon as she could, she was going to do her best to meet some real person who just might become a friend. At least a friendly acquaintance. And she'd buy some flowers for the flower beds. It was too cold to be planting anything, but she would check at the garden center and do what she could anyway. The as yet unknown Plumber was kind enough to let her use his cottage. The least she could do would be to plant some bulbs or get some flower seeds to plant when it warmed up.

Gabby grunted. Likely he wouldn't care either way. But

she did. It'd be her first mark in her new life. Maybe planting some flowers wasn't much of a legacy, but it was something.

And sometimes any something was better than every nothing.

CHAPTER FOURTEEN

Friday, December 11, 11:50 a.m.

THE THIRD PACKAGE arrived just before noon. It wasn't delivered by a traditional carrier. It was a woman about Gabby's age with long brown hair that was sun-burnished from the ear down to the ends and hung low on her shoulders. She was pretty, and she smiled a lot. Quickly, she identified herself. "Hi, Gabby. I'm Kelly Meyer, Plumber's younger sister."

Surmising she'd readied the cottage, Gabby nodded and attempted a smile. "Hi."

Standing on the porch, she didn't move forward or signal she wanted to be let inside. "I intercepted the Fed Ex driver on the way in. I hope you don't mind." Kelly passed a bulky padded envelope. "Do you have any coffee made? I just pulled an all-nighter at the station and I need a boost of caffeine to make it home."

She wore a cop's uniform. Gabby was torn. Did she let her in or not? If she was Plumber's sister, she was trustworthy but also a local cop, and she drove a Jeep, not a cruiser. Still, how dangerous could she be? "Sure, come in. I just put on a fresh pot."

Kelly walked straight through to the kitchen, opened the right cabinet door and pulled out a mug, then poured. "I hope the groceries are okay. I wasn't sure what you'd like, so I tried to get a little bit of everything."

She'd guessed right. "You stocked the fridge and pantry?" Gabby stood watching her. Kelly seemed so at ease and comfortable. Clearly, she knew her way around the cottage.

"I did." She took her cup and sat down at the breakfast bar. "Plumber said you'd be arriving late and needing some supplies."

"That was kind of you, Kelly." Gabby filled her mug and stood across the bar from her. "Thank you." Her face reddened. "I need to repay you for the groceries."

"Plumber already did." She waved Gabby off. "I didn't come out to intercept your package. I came because Plumber mentioned you might need a few clothing items to hold you over for a few days until you could get into town to shop."

That had to have raised Kelly's curiosity. Gabby wondered what the woman thought of it. Before she could work her way around to finding out, Kelly spilled her thoughts.

"Leaving an abusive relationship with no notice . . . That had to be hard."

"I'm sure it's never easy." Gabby put the package on the counter by the stove. Did that qualify as a lie by omission? She didn't actually say she'd been in an abusive relationship, though in a sense her relationship with her father did qualify. That was a thin-line quandary. Honesty, she valued. But lying grated at Gabby. She supposed she didn't have a lot of choice, considering telling anyone the truth could put them in jeopardy, too. She had enough guilt on her plate without adding that.

Kelly looked Gabby over. "You're about the same size as Sara Cramer. Or maybe Lys Hayden."

"Who are they?" Gabby took a sip of her coffee, thinking she'd give her eye teeth for a cup of Earl Grey White Tip tea. She would *not* give that up, too.

"Sara does beautiful floral designs. She has a shop on the Cove. Sara—not Sara's—Blossoms. Actually, she has flowers and a gardening center." Kelly paused to drink from her mug. "Lys Hayden is a conservationist. She's in law enforcement, too. Keeps an eye on wildlife and the preserve east of town. They're both good people and my lifelong friends. We all grew up together here." Kelly pulled out her phone. "I need just a sec."

Gabby motioned she would step away, but Kelly said, "No, you're fine." She spoke into the phone. "Sara, I need some clothes. Just a couple casual outfits—enough for a few days. Plumber's friend—yes, Gabby. That's her. Anyway, she had to leave with nothing, and all the stores are closed today." Kelly tilted the phone and told Gabby. "Gearing up for the Christmas Festival. It's tomorrow night, so today's an off day for almost everyone, so they can help setup. The residents cut a deal with Pastor Brown. You know, to keep attendance up at Sunday's service."

Post festival weariness, Gabby supposed. She nodded, having no idea what to say or do.

"I was thinking that, too," Kelly said into the phone. "We'll see you in half an hour, then."

Half an hour? Gabby swallowed hard. How could she keep up this conversation for half an hour?

Kelly stowed her phone. "Sara's calling Lys and they'll bring you some emergency gear." She shrugged. "I have no idea what to expect. Lys tromps around in overalls and muddy boots most of the time and Sara in jeans and t-shirts, but at least they won't be too big for you."

Gabby's face heated. "I borrowed some clothes I found in the closet."

"Plumber's," Kelly said. "That explains the cuffs on the sleeves and pant legs." She laughed. "He's a big guy."

He was. Kelly's laugh wasn't degrading, but it was infectious. Gabby laughed with her. "I'm grateful for them." She worried her lip. "I should have thought to stop and get some on the road, but it didn't even cross my mind."

"I expect your mind was right where it needed to be—on getting away. When someone is in that fight-or-flight state, clothes are the last of their worries."

"True." That's as far as Gabby could go.

"You need to sit down, Gabby." Kelly lifted a hand and rubbed her nape. "I'm getting a crick in my neck."

"Sorry." Gabby tugged a stool to her side of the bar. She didn't feel at all threatened by Kelly, but a little distance was in order. Now this Sara and Lys were coming to the cottage and it'd be three against one. Gabby didn't like her odds on that, but she had a feeling Kelly was exactly who she presented herself to be, and if she was Plumber's sister . . .

But what if she wasn't?

Kelly filled the time putting Gabby at ease. Giving her directions to the shops on the cove, telling her where to get her hair and nails done, and where to buy groceries.

"Is there a tea shop?" Gabby asked.

"Actually, no, there isn't." Kelly grunted. "Apple cider, coffee, and that kind of thing, but no tea shop. Maybe Alyce at the coffee shop could order in for you."

Gabby ventured to present a little of herself. Well, her new self. "Maybe I'll add teas to my little business."

That surprised Kelly. "You've got a business?"

"Not yet. But I'm planning one." Gabby took the leap. "I want to make soaps and maybe bath oils and lotions. And I love exotic teas." She winced. "That's an odd combination though, isn't it?"

"I don't see anything odd about it." Kelly fluffed her hair then flipped it behind her shoulder. "Shoot, why not make it a hodgepodge of things you love kind of shop?"

"I've never heard of that of that kind of shop."

"It'd be the first of its kind in the Cove." Kelly refilled her cup. "Fill your shop only with things you love, no matter what they are."

Clearly, Kelly liked the idea. Gabby wasn't sold on it being a recipe for success. "That might make it hard for shoppers. They won't know what to expect."

Kelly set the coffee carafe back on its burner and grunted. "You say that as if it's a bad thing."

"Isn't it?" It flew in the face of conventional wisdom. No marketer in the world would agree uncertainty was a good idea. And yet . . .

"I think shoppers, particularly women, love to be surprised now and then. It's like a Christmas Stocking." Kelly returned to her seat. "You never know what you're going to find in it, but you know it'll be something special."

"Or fun."

"Or frivolous. Women love frivolous, but feel guilty buying, which of course, they do anyway." Kelly's eyes twinkled. "Your shop could be famous for spousal makeup gifts."

"Famous for restoring the peace." For shoppers and for Gabby.

"Famous for getting hubby out of the doghouse." Kelly laughed hard and deep. "You'll make a fortune."

"I like that restoring the peace," Gabby admitted. "It seems awfully self-indulgent and risky, but it sounds like fun, too."

"Soaps and teas and—and whatever else Gabby treasures."

Gabby stilled. That was it. The name of her business.

"Gabby's Treasures." She smiled. "Kelly, you're a genius." The smile grew to a laugh, but steel determination settled under it. Mentally, she added it to her list. "One day, I am going to open a shop and call it Gabby's Treasures."

Kelly's eyes sparkled. "Awesome. There happens to be a little place for lease in the business district."

"I'm probably going to have to build an online business first to earn enough to fund an actual store."

"Starting from scratch. I forgot. Sorry." Kelly looked genuinely contrite. "Well, it just so happens the place is empty and it's not doing anyone any good—the other merchants do not like to see empty stores. Let me talk to the owner and see if there's anything he can do."

"Who is the owner?"

"Plumber." Kelly grinned.

"Oh, no. Don't do that." Gabby set down her cup. "He's letting me stay here already. And I don't have the funds to stock the place right now, so there's no sense in it."

Kelly nodded.

"Do you live in the farmhouse next door?"

"No, our folks do, when they're not traveling." Kelly grinned. "That's not often these days, though they do usually make it home once a year for a week or two."

"So they love to travel."

"Mom does," Kelly said. "Dad tolerates it because he loves her. He'd be planted on this property if it were just up to him. But he promised her they could travel, so when he retired, they bought a big RV and they've been on the road most of the time since."

Gabby chuckled. "He's enjoying it or he'd never be doing that."

"Exactly." Kelly nodded her agreement, then sipped at her coffee.

A knock on the door interrupted their conversation.

Kelly jumped to her feet. "Sara and Lys," she said. "I'll get it."

Gabby checked the clock. Thirty minutes had passed already? She couldn't believe it.

Sara and Lys came in with their arms full of clothes and dumped them on the sofa. Which was which, Gabby didn't have a clue. Not until she looked at their shoes.

Lys wore boots—no mud. And a tan cap. Her sandy-blond hair was long, loose and curly, and her eyes bright and intelligent. Sara was a redhead, tiny and delicate looking. It was just a feeling, but Gabby thought that fragile look might be deceptive.

"Hi, Gabby. I'm Sara," the redhead said.

"I'm Lys Hayden," the blonde in boots said. "Glad to meet you."

"We didn't know what style you like, though neither of us has much in the way of stylish clothes, but we grabbed what we had, and you're welcome to it."

The gesture overwhelmed Gabby. Yes, the thought had crossed her mind that she'd been found and this could be a way Medros had wheedled his way in to kill her—she'd been warned the assassin could be anyone—but it was highly unlikely they'd come in as Christmas Cove locals, gifting her with clothes.

Kelly's phone rang. "Oh, that's Plumber." She stepped away. "Hey, brother. What's up?"

She listened for a moment while Gabby got Lys and Sara coffee, then Kelly said, "We're at the cottage with Gabby right now."

Hearing Kelly speak Gabby's name caught her ear.

"Hang on a second. I'll get her for you." Kelly walked over and offered the phone. "Plumber wants to say hi."

Gabby clasped it from Kelly. Her throat tightened. "Hello."

"You okay or has the triple threat driven you up the wall already?"

Shadow Watcher. She'd know his voice anywhere. He was Plumber. "I was—"

"Freaking out that they might not be who they said they were. I can imagine you were. And Kelly comes on like gangbusters. Not a subtle gene in her. Sara's more tranquil. Lys is tough, blunt but fair. I figured you'd have another day before she descended on you with the group of them, but then I remembered this was Kelly. So, I thought I'd better call and put your mind at ease."

"I appreciate that, and you have." The man was incredibly thoughtful and kind and so much more. She now had two names for him—Shadow Watcher and Plumber—and she still didn't know his real name but made a mental note to only refer to him as Plumber to Kelly, Sara and Lys.

"Did you get the package today?"

"Yes. Kelly intercepted the Fed Ex driver and brought it in with her."

He sighed. "Guess I should be glad she didn't open it. She didn't, did she?"

Gabby smiled. "It's not opened."

"Wait until they've gone. It's a second phone for just us and some additional paper we dropped so your paper trail didn't seem sparse when compared to other average people."

"I will. Thanks for . . . everything." Smart move, adding to the trail. Nothing stuck out in research so much as the absence of stuff. Every life had stuff.

"Soon."

See you soon? Talk to you soon? He had to mean they would talk soon. "Soon."

The line went dead and she passed the phone back to Kelly. "Thank you."

Lys snagged a mug of coffee and inhaled deeply. "I love

the idea for Gabby's Treasures."

Kelly had told them. And they were excited. Gabby wasn't sure what to do with that. "It's just a dream at this point."

"Every dream is just a dream at the beginning," Sara said. "I love special teas, but I'm not crazy about driving into St. Louis to get them. Having them in Christmas Cove would be fabulous. Your shop will fit right in."

"I hate that drive, too," Lys chimed in. "Besides, Gabby, every dream is an adventure. What's not to love about an adventure?" Lys shrugged. "Do you love peppermint soap? I hope you do because I love it. The good kind—real peppermint oil." She scrunched her mouth into a grimace. "The fake stuff just doesn't hack it."

"I'll make some especially for you, using only the best," Gabby said, feeling excitement well inside her. Not just about the shop, though there was plenty of that, too. But even more, she was a stranger to dreams and adventures. And to these women. Yet here they sat offering her encouragement and support.

This is what friends did. This is what having friends was like.

It was an alien feeling. A magnificent feeling.

Deeply moved at getting to experience it, Gabby's eyes blurred.

"Hey, are you okay, Gabby?" Sara looked at her, concern in her expression and her voice.

Gabby nodded, debated on how honest to be, and decided to jump in all the way. "I'm moved. You are all so kind and good and supportive. I've never known that."

Kelly frowned. "Abusers often see to that. They love isolating their victims."

"I've heard that." Sara sipped at her coffee.

Lys looked hard at Gabby. "So, he isolated you from other people? Friends and everything?"

"I've never had friends," Gabby admitted, choosing her words carefully. "Or, to be honest, everything."

"Ever?" Lys raised her voice. "Not even when you were a kid?"

"Ever." Gabby cringed, feeling vulnerable and exposed, but she forced herself to push on. "Sometimes you self-isolate because you don't want anyone else to know your family secrets."

Sara started to say something, but Kelly raised a hand, silencing her. "Why not, Gabby?"

Her mouth went dry. This "all in" business was harder than giving up the Mustang. She tried but failed to meet Kelly's eyes, focused just beyond her shoulder to the wall behind her, but seeing far beyond it and into her past. "Because you're ashamed."

"Of what?" Lys asked, claiming Gabby's gaze. "Glare at me all you want, Kelly. I want to know."

Gabby took a drink of coffee and set her cup firmly on the bar. "Being unlovable." Even to her, her voice sounded reed thin and weak.

"That's crazy, Gabby," Lys belted out. "You're beautiful and smart and you make good coffee. I know people who have built friendships on a lot less than that."

"True." Sara grunted. "Shoot, I know someone who married on less than that."

"You don't," Kelly said. When Sara nodded, insisting she did, Kelly gasped. "Who?"

"My mother." Sara bobbed her head. "She said my dad had a nice smile. She married him for his smile."

"Humph." Kelly grunted. "You know, I can see that. Your mom has a serious nature. A good smile would be important to her." Kelly swerved her gaze back to Gabby. "You're lovable, Gabby, and don't you believe anyone who tells you different. Ever. It's a straight up lie."

"That's right." Lys said with an emphatic nod.

"Absolutely." Sara sniffed, clearly affronted at the notion.

Gabby didn't know what to say. They barely knew her yet defended her. "Thank you. Seriously." Her throat went tight. "I'll, um, try to remember that."

"No problem." Lys drained her cup. "If you forget, we'll remind you." She made her way to the coffeepot for a refill. "Friends do that."

Sara grunted. "Friends have to do that, or those old tapes that run in our heads would drive us nuts."

"True." Kelly nodded her agreement. "Remember when I went through that phase?"

"Which one?" Lys asked.

"Ugly. I was totally and irredeemably ugly, inside and out."

"Ugh! Do I ever," Sara said. "She was a hot mess, Gabby, and clearly there wasn't a drop of truth in it. But her dad said it, and so she believed it."

"Dads don't lie, and they love you," Kelly said. "Of course, I believed it."

Sara dipped her chin, slid Kelly a knowing look. "Dads also disapprove of their daughter's dying their hair green for St. Patrick's Day and overreact."

"I think the henna tattoo of a four-leaf clover on your face bothered him more than the green hair," Lys chimed in. "Honestly, he hated them both. The combination overwhelmed him, and he popped his cork." She shrugged. "It happens."

If you forget, we'll remind you. Friends do that . . .

Gabby could scarcely believe it. They'd taken her in. Just that fast, she was one of them. All her life she'd craved just one friend. And in her new life, in the span of a few hours, she had three.

Forget irony. Life mystified her.

And she liked it.

CHAPTER FIFTEEN

Monday, December 14, 9:30 p.m.

GABBY SAT at the bar refining a recipe for peppermint soap. Her grandmother's recipes were time-tested and perfect. Unfortunately, she hadn't memorized them. Some of the oils and supplies she'd ordered had arrived, but then she'd found a familiar named peppermint oil that could be the one in her grandmother's book. As soon as it arrived, she intended to make another test batch of soaps with it for Lys. She'd give Gabby her blunt and frank opinion. Friends were just invaluable for that. They didn't sugar-coat a thing.

Lifting her glass of milk, Gabby took a sip and debated eating a brownie she'd baked that afternoon. She'd made several batches of soaps and of brownies to take with her tomorrow, thinking the festival workers might enjoy samples of the soaps and a snack. It could help her get to know some of the residents. Sometime during her days there and interactions with the triple threat, she decided she wanted a life here among them, and she meant to become one of them.

The doorbell rang.

Gabby nearly dropped her glass. *Medros?* Shaking, she set the glass down and moved toward the door, heard a man on the porch mumbling. She peeked out.

"It's me, Gabby," he said, looking right at her.

She didn't know his face, but his voice . . . "Shadow—" she started.

"Plumber," he cut her off. "It's Plumber."

Gabby opened the door, her every nerve fraying. "What's wrong?"

He stepped inside, shut then locked the door and finally grabbed her into a hug. "Thank God. Thank God, you're all right."

His crisp scent surrounded her. She hugged him back. It was the most wonderful hug she'd felt in her life. "Why wouldn't I be all right?" she asked, pinned against his shoulder. Then she recalled they'd had a close call while she was on the road. "Did the close call develop into a problem?"

"No, we handled it." His breath warm on her neck, he didn't let her go. A slight tremble coursed through his huge body.

She reared back, looked up into his handsome face. His hair was light brown with golden streaks, his beard short and stubbled as men seemed to favor right now, but his eyes . . . his eyes stole her breath. Green and deep and, at the moment, clouded with worry. He was tall and muscular, lean like an athlete rather than the computer geek locked in an office all the time she'd imagined him. "Plumber, what's wrong? Why are you here?"

He stepped back and actually smiled. "A couple of reasons," he said. "I'm home for Christmas. And I wanted to see with my own eyes that you're okay. The whole time you were on the road, I was a wreck. Oh, and I bring good news on your assets, which I am happy to report have been deposited into your new bank account."

Her heart lurched. "I have a new bank account?"

"Gabby Johnson does indeed have a new fat account. It routes through—never mind. You'll see all that on the transaction report. The important thing is the deposits eventually wind up here at First National Bank in the Cove. It's on First and Main. Very convenient."

She'd seen it on her trips to town. Her mind jumped into mental gymnastics. "So, if I write a check, then anyone can track me here?"

"No, they can't, because funds funnel out the same route in reverse." He stepped away and tousled the hair over his right ear. "It appears Gabby Johnson is in the Caribbean."

That relieved her. "Thank you."

"You're welcome." He shrugged out of his black jacket and smiled. "Why am I smelling brownies?"

"I spent part of the day baking them. Want one?"

"I'd love one." He sniffed. "I'm smelling peppermint, too."

"I've been making soap, too."

"Great." He walked over to the breakfast bar, then hung his jacket on the back of the barstool. "You haven't asked how good the news is on your assets."

She served them both brownies and him a glass of milk. "Honestly, I'm afraid to ask." Enough for an online store beginning, or a brick-and-mortar store, or both? She had no idea what to expect.

"There's no need for fear."

"Seriously?"

He nodded. "I told you it was good news. We were largely successful."

That surprised her. "How did you make that happen?"

An enigmatic smile curved his broad mouth. "You don't want to know."

"TreasureSeeker can be very creative," she said, figuring

that member of Troop Search and Rescue would take the lead on asset recovery. He typically did.

"Very creative." Plumber confirmed it. "He couldn't do much on the house or your apartment, but if your Aunt Janelle is still alive—Hunter is all over that—she'll be shocked about your father and you, but if she's been in a financial struggle, she'll be relieved."

"I hope she isn't—having financial problems, I mean."

"She was fine until a couple of years ago. Then her business went south—a string of gyms mostly in lower income areas. ThumpIt says she provided too many low-cost memberships, trying to help people get healthier."

ThumpIt was an excellent investigator. He would know, but . . . "Memberships wouldn't cost her much, so that doesn't quite make sense to me."

Shadow—Plumber shot her a knowing look. "It does when you factor in all the loans she made to her members."

"What kind of loans?" Gabby asked, then took a bite of rich, chocolate brownie.

"Groceries, rent, utilities, childcare—whatever they needed."

"Admirable." A spark of pride in her aunt flared to life.

"Yes, but she was too generous. She failed to take care to provide for herself, which means now she's not there to help herself or anyone else."

Gabby hated to hear that. "You think she's still alive, then?"

Empathy flashed across his face. "To be determined. Hunter is still looking. After the gyms closed, she sold her house and seemingly disappeared."

Fear flashed through Gabby. "You don't think—"

"Don't go there." He held up a hand. "We have found no reason Medros would go after her. There's no evidence that he even knew she existed."

Gabby's hand went to her chest to calm her pounding heart. "I found some letters from her. In one, she said she knew my father kept her away from me because she knew too much, so it's natural my mind would go there."

"Too much about what?"

"I have no idea. She didn't say."

Plumber reached back into his jacket and pulled out a brown envelope then passed it over to Gabby. "Your asset info, transaction report, and some temporary checks. The bank is sending you a supply."

She took the envelope with a trembling hand. Her future lay in what was in this envelope. Had they recovered enough to give her a new start? He'd said the troops had been very successful. But had TreasureSeeker even found her trust fund? Her 401K?

"You need to review the list and make sure we got everything. If we missed something, we might still be able to retrieve it."

She steeled herself and opened the envelope. Reviewed the neat spreadsheet, item by item. Her heart thudded faster and faster and her eyes burned then blurred. "You got it all." Her entire portfolio of liquid assets was included. All of it! She dropped the paper onto the bar, came around and hugged him hard. "Thank you. Oh, thank you!"

He pulled her to him and held her. "I thought that would make you happy, but if I'd known it'd get you into my arms, I'd have told TreasureSeeker to hustle even more."

She stilled, pulled back and met his gaze. "You want me in your arms?"

He studied her face a long moment. "More than my next breath."

His sincerity warmed her, thrilled her. "I do like it here."

"In Christmas Cove?" he asked.

"Yes, but that's not what I meant." She was terrified but

took the leap. "In your arms." Was it possible to come to care so much for someone you knew for five years but didn't really know?

"I like you here, too."

"In Christmas Cove or—"

"Both." He leaned forward and covered her lips in a tender kiss.

Apparently, it was possible. She cupped his face in her hands and kissed him back.

GABBY AND PLUMBER talked and talked, moved to the sofa with glasses of wine, and talked some more. He was charming, as blunt as Lys, and he had a wicked sense of humor that appealed to Gabby on so many levels she couldn't even label them all. And not once did it occur to her to not just relax and speak freely. By his actions and deeds, he had proven if there was anything to know about her, he already knew it. No secrets and nothing to hide was new to her, and she'd often yearned for someone to share with like this, but never had she dared to think, much less to dream, she'd actually find it. Yet, she had in him.

Finally, he sat back. "I'm glad you like Christmas Cove."

"What's not to like? It's beautiful and cheerful and the people are amazing."

"You went to town."

"I did." A couple of times. She couldn't not smile. "Kelly and Sara showed me around. Lys was on the mountain checking out a poacher complaint."

"She gets those from time to time."

"Sara told me."

"So, they trotted you around and introduced you to everyone."

"If there's anyone they missed, I don't know who it would be." Gabby chuckled. "Most of them seemed to know about me before we met."

"That's one of the challenges of a small town and, frankly, why I spend so much time away from home."

The secrets he keeps from them.

"That must be hard for you."

"Sometimes it is. You've seen how close family and friends are here. I miss that. But then there are other times when I know I need to do what I'm doing."

Helping people like her. "It makes a difference." She wouldn't be alive without him and the troops. She had no illusions about that. Medros's henchmen would have killed her the night her father's house exploded.

"It does. At least, more often than it doesn't. I'll take those results." He nodded. "How is the new-life plan coming along?"

"It was tough to get started, to tell you the truth. But once I made a monumental mind shift, I started making progress. Now, I'm making big strides—which I need to adjust to include all the assets you guys recovered."

Uncertainty had the skin between his eyebrows crinkled. "Is that a good or bad thing?"

"It's a great thing," she assured him. "I have options and choices I only dreamed of before now."

"Gabby dreaming. I like that." He smiled. "I'm eager to hear all about your plans, but first, there's something I have to know for purely selfish reasons."

"What's that?"

"During this tour of the Cove where you met everyone in the area, how many jobs did you get sucked into for the festival?"

She laughed. "A couple."

"Knew it." He slapped his jean-clad knee.

"I got recruited to help decorate the pier for the blessing of the boats."

"The fleet," he said. "It's the blessing of the fleet."

"Right."

"Kelly?"

"Lys," Gabby corrected him, took a tiny sip of wine. "Kelly snagged me for two hours, manning the hot-chocolate stand during the bonfire."

"That's a popular spot then. You'll be busy." He chuckled. "What did Sara snag you for?"

"How did you know she did?"

"I know them well." He pursed his lips. "Triple threat. Always."

"They're wonderful."

"I agree." He rubbed the rim of his stemmed glass with his thumb. "The good news is they really like you or none of them would have recruited you at all. The bad news is because they like you, you'll be drafted onto every volunteer project from now on."

Gabby laughed. "I kind of like that idea." He seemed a little perplexed. She shrugged. "When you have no one, having a lot of someones, even ones who don't know you well, is special." A gift truly, but maybe you had to walk in those shoes to really understand that.

"You should be thrilled then. Just remember, 'No is a complete sentence'."

She marked an "X" over her chest. "I will."

"Great. So tell me more about your new-life plan."

"That's the best part. Well, it could be the best part. It depends on whether or not you'd mind me putting down roots here."

"Seriously?"

"I love it here, Plumber." She had to remind herself to stick with that name. In her mind, she always thought

Shadow Watcher or SW first and then switched to Plumber. The last thing he needed was for her to blow his cover in his hometown. "It's everything I always wanted and maybe more than I knew I could want. Wonderful things. But I don't want to intrude on your turf, so if you have any objection, just let me know."

"Why would I object?"

"Having anyone around who knows the other world you walk in . . ." She let her voice fade and shrugged.

"Gabby, no. I totally trust you." He lifted a fingertip to her chin, slid it along her jaw. "I'm happy you're here, and even happier you want to stay."

Her relief was immediate and intense. "Thank you." She clasped his hand and gave it a gentle squeeze.

"You weren't kidding. You're moving at the speed of light if you have your plan worked out to the point you know you want to stay here."

"I am and I do." She smiled, then worried her lower lip with her teeth. "It wasn't a risk assessment or logical decision." He'd probably laugh at her for that. "The triple threat welcomed me, went out of their way to help and treated me . . ."

He didn't laugh, but his voice did soften. "Like a friend?" he guessed.

She nodded. "Then everyone in town was so kind. I've never had that, and I've always wanted it."

"So, what you're saying is you've made your decisions based on emotion." He paused, weighed that and when she nodded, he added, "Is this life one you will love?"

"I will totally love it," she said, looking him right in the eye. "I already do."

"This just keeps getting better and better." Genuinely happy, he pressed her for more details. "What do you have in mind?"

Gabby could barely contain her excitement. "I want a shop on Main Street."

"What kind of shop?"

"Selling handmade soaps and lotions and bath crystals and exotic teas and whatever else I come across that I love."

"That's an interesting line of products."

"I know they're disparate, but I think I can make it work. I will only carry things I love. Life's little indulgences. Nothing too expensive but those little touches that make us feel pampered and nurtured and loved."

"All the things you didn't feel, growing up."

"Yes." She answered honestly. "I'm going to call it Gabby's Treasures."

He studied her face. "You're really excited about this."

"I am. Christmas Cove is a perfect market for what I have in mind, and I can do online sales, too. It'll be awesome. Some of the locals expressed interest in carrying my products —if I had to build online before opening a store on Main Street. But thanks to you and the troops, I can launch the Main Street store right away. Even Pastor Ruther says it can work."

"Pastor Ruther?" That seemed to surprise Plumber.

She nodded. "On the rare occasion, he needs a get-out-of-the-doghouse gift for Mrs. Ruther."

Plumber laughed. "I hadn't thought of that angle. I can see it," Plumber added. "He's a bit of a cynic now and then."

"Aren't we all?"

"Pretty much." Plumber drank, then set his glass back down on the coffee table. "Considering the dog-house angle, I predict Gabby's Treasures will be a huge success."

"Do you really think so?"

"You love it, Gabby. You'll make it work."

"I will." She studied his face. "You're loving this."

"Honestly, yeah. I am."

"Why?"

"It makes you happy."

"And that pleases you?"

"It does." He let out a little grunt. "You have no idea how much time I've invested in the past five years wondering what it would take for you to be happy."

Her heart lurched. "Why?" He constantly surprised her.

"Because you should be happy. It makes me happy to see you happy. To think of you being content and happy." He stood up. "In fact, I have a surprise for you that's going to make you even happier."

"I don't know if that's possible. I'm bursting at the seams already."

"Oh, it will." His eyes lit with a beautiful little twinkle. "I'll bet on it."

She tilted her head. "What's the bet?"

He thought half a beat, then suggested, "A kiss?"

As if that would be a hardship. Women would stand in line. "You're on."

He walked over to the door. Was he leaving? No, he stopped and retrieved something from the narrow table near the door, atop of a stack of books. A wrapped package with a big red bow. How had she missed seeing that?

Walking back over, he passed her the box. "For you."

A gift. On top of everything else, he'd gotten her a gift? "Should I open it now?" Part of her wanted to rip into the package, but another part of her, that part that had spent so many Christmases alone, wanted to wait for Christmas morning.

"Absolutely now."

That settled it. "Okay." Carefully, she removed the ribbon, her hand shaking. Green tissue paper inside. She couldn't imagine what lay beneath it. Whatever it was, it had some weight to it. Easing a fingertip between the sheets, she folded the paper back . . . "Oh, Plumber." She couldn't believe her eyes. Tears surged up from deep inside and clogged her throat. "My Grandmother's book of soap recipes?" She fingered through the pages of soaps and the sections for lotions and oils, all of which Gabby had dreamed about, imagined making, and noting the little tick marks beside the ones she had made—and seen in her mind's eye, her and her grandmother there in her kitchen, reading the same recipes, measuring the same ingredients, shaping the same soaps with her hands that Gabby shaped with her own. She'd never met her grandmother, but she had come to know her through this book, through their shared passion for creating soaps with care and love. Gabby swallowed hard, blinked rapidly, but the tears leaked anyway and slid down her cheeks. "I thought I'd never see these again." She sniffed and looked up at him.

The look on his face grew tender. "It meant the most to you."

It did. "How did you get it?"

"A minor case of breaking and entering. You really should not leave a key in one of those rocks at the foot of the stairs to your front door, Gabby. Everyone knows about those rocks, and it was the only one around."

"But the alarm?"

"A little bypass on the system. I reset it when I left."

She sniffed again, swiped at her tears with her napkin. "You are definitely a man of many talents." She stood and hugged him hard, then stepped back. "Thank you so much."

"You're welcome." He lifted his arms. "You look pretty happy."

"Oh, I am."

He smiled. "Then I believe that means I won the bet."

She set the box aside, stood and walked into his waiting arms. "And that means I owe you a kiss."

"A real one, not a peck. Your neighbor's dog threatened to come across the fence at me."

"Bruiser is not a friendly pup."

"He's not a pup. He's a Great Dane nearly the size of a small horse, and he could rip my head off."

"Probably could." She kissed him deeply, then pulled back and kissed him again, losing herself in sensation.

"Two kisses. For that, I'd risk Bruiser again. Anything else you want from there?"

"Afraid not," she said softly. "Everything I want is right here."

The look in his eyes warmed. "I knew it'd be like this between us."

Gabby let him see the truth in her own eyes. "I hoped it would be."

"I'm glad to know that." He hugged her to him. A long second later, he pulled away. "Really glad." He cupped her face in his hands. "On that high note, I need to go."

"Okay." Her disappointment must have showed.

"I have to be on Main Street at 9:30 in the morning."

"Ah, so you've been recruited, too." The smile in her heart touched her eyes.

"Every year," he confessed. "I help Pastor Ruther set up the podium for the blessing of the fleet." Plumber stepped away and retrieved his jacket from the chair at the breakfast bar. "What time do you have to be there?"

"Nine-thirty. I'm helping Kelly and Lys put some fencing on the dock. Kelly's worried the little ones could step off and into the water."

"That's because when she was a little one, she did."

"You went in after her."

"Actually, I did." He shivered. "That water was so cold."

"I'll bet."

He paused. "Want to ride in together?"

"Sure."

"That'll work." Plumber shrugged into his jacket. "I'll be here at 9:15."

That confused her. "Where are you staying?"

"In the farmhouse next door."

"Of course. I'll walk over."

He started toward the door.

"By the way," she said. "Who do I owe for the Malibu?"

"No one. The Mustang took care of it."

"But the Mustang was totaled in the crash." Now, she was really confused.

"I couldn't do it," he confessed, doing his best to look sheepish. "You loved that car."

She had. But that mattering to him surprised her. "So, what car crashed in the accident where I died?"

"A Mustang."

He'd switched the vehicles. That explained how it had gotten to Florida so fast. "And Medros's goons inspected it and thought it was mine?"

He nodded. "Simple change of VIN plate, tags, and such."

The troops had gone to a lot of extra trouble. She almost felt guilty about that. Almost. But guilt paled compared to knowing her Mustang survived even if she hadn't. "Where's my Mustang?"

He smiled enigmatically. "Safely tucked away for another day."

A little laugh escaped her. "All I can say is, if a body has to die to live, you and the troops are definitely the people to have on your side, making it happen."

He winked. "For the troops, it's anything for our Gate Keeper."

Plumber had excluded himself. She didn't know what to think about that.

"For me, it's anything for you." He winked at her then walked toward the door and said over his shoulder. "Lock it."

She walked over and locked the door, grinning like an idiot, happier than she'd ever been in her life.

Amazing. Just amazing. Who could have imagined that life after death—okay, life after fake death—could be so good? So full of promise for everything her heart ever had desired?

It was a miracle.

Her Grandmother's book of soap recipes *and* her Mustang spared and safe?

More miracles.

And Shadow Watcher—er, Plumber?

Okay, hands down, a fistful of miracles.

CHAPTER SIXTEEN

Tuesday, December 15, 9:00 a.m.

GABBY HAD TESTED her first batch of soaps twice and they'd made the cut. She inserted them in the sample packaging she had ordered and dropped them into colorful Christmas gift bags. The brownies she'd loaded into Christmas tins and stacked them on the end of the breakfast bar.

Rushing to get a second cup of coffee down before 9:10, she rinsed the cup at the sink, put on her hat, coat and gloves and scooped up the goodies, then headed for the door. As she reached for the doorknob, she heard someone knocking. Startled, she juggled the tins and spilled them onto the side-table to keep from dropping them. How long would it take to stop jumping out of her skin every time someone came to the door?

"Gabby, it's me."

Plumber. Her heart got out of her throat and back into her chest where it belonged. She opened the door. "Good morning."

"I'm early."

Like her, he'd dressed in jeans and a heavy sweater under his coat. "Three minutes or so, but I'm ready." She reached for the brownie tins on the little table.

He wiggled a fingertip between the giftbags looped at her wrist to the tins. "What's all this?"

"Sample soaps and brownies." She passed the stack of tins to him. "The soaps are promised, and I thought the workers might like a snack."

"The people here are going to love you," he predicted. "One thing Christmas Covers love almost as much as the holidays is food."

She laughed. "Christmas Covers. Is that what the residents call themselves?"

"Typically, it's just Covers."

"That's a clever way to differentiate between locals and tourists."

"I guess. Never really thought about it. Just grew up with it, you know?"

She had no idea what that was like but nodded anyway.

They locked up then went outside and climbed into his white Jeep. "Who did you promise the soaps?" he asked.

Gabby clicked her seatbelt into place. "Alyce Crawley at the coffeeshop, Mimi Taylor—she crafts the best ornaments, doesn't she?"

"The kids love decorating their own. The adults, too, for that matter." He cranked the engine and put the Jeep into Drive.

"And Leigh Pace at Patchwork Needle." Her quilts and quilted items were unusual and just gorgeous.

"And the rest?" he asked. "I'm counting six bags." He pulled onto the road to the business district and headed toward Main Street and the docks that were located at the foot of it.

"The triple threat." The Jeep hit a bump, and Gabby grabbed the door.

"I'll go with you to make the deliveries."

"I don't want to slow you down."

Plumber shrugged. "You won't."

The stores were less than a block apart, so the deliveries went swiftly. "I have an ulterior motive for going with you," Plumber said. "I want to show you something."

"Okay." Gabby had no idea what to expect. It seemed everyone here knew and liked him. All three of the women, Alyce, Mimi and Leigh, had hugged and chastised him for staying gone so long this time. Alyce actually had told Gabby she needed to see to it he came home more often. That flustered Gabby. Why would Alyce think Gabby had any control over Plumber's schedule or activities?

At the corner of Main and First, across the street from the bank, he pulled to the curb. "We're here."

Her heart pounded hard. He'd parked directly in front of the little store with the wide front window and the old-fashioned green door. She loved that storefront. On first sight, she had imagined Gabby's Treasures there.

"When you were talking about your store, this place came to mind. It's empty. I thought you could take a look." He walked right to the door and inserted an old skeleton key into the lock. "What would you think about opening Gabby's Treasures here?"

She stepped inside. A long wooden counter stretched halfway down the right side of the expanse. A few shelves hung stacked on the wall behind it, and the backside of the counter was all cabinets for storage. The rest of the shop was empty. White walls, tile floor—a blank slate. Almost breathless, Gabby said, "It's on Main and First."

"You said in the business district," Plumber reminded her, sounding uncertain. "Do you like it?"

She paused and turned to face him, her emotions in riot. "This is the shop I dreamed on, Plumber."

"Nightmare or good dream?" He stuffed a hand into his jacket pocket. "I'm not sure what you mean."

"When I was here earlier, I stood on the sidewalk and looked in through the window, and I imagined exactly what I wanted my store to look like. I promised myself that one day I'd have a brick-and-mortar Gabby's Treasures here."

"So, you do like it, then?" He relaxed and walked around the counter, then leaned against it and watched her walk around and dream some more.

"It's perfect." She shimmied her delight. "I love it."

"I had a feeling you would. Well, I hoped you would." He smiled. "It so happens I own it."

Gabby spun to face him. "You own this building?" Kelly had mentioned he owned a storefront, but not this one. Gabby'd had no idea.

"This store, yes."

"And you'll sell it to me?"

"No, it's not for sale, but I'll give you a long-term or a short-term lease. Whatever you want."

Gabby squealed her delight and rounded the corner to hug him. "Thank you, Plumber."

"It's good for me, too. Empty shops on Main Street make for lousy business. Everyone hates that." He chuckled. "But I do love seeing you happy, Gabby."

"I am ecstatically happy." She looked up at him. "Do you have a list of my dreams or something?"

"Do you have a list of your dreams?"

"I do now." She cocked her head. "It's as if you know what I want before I know it, and you somehow make it happen. I find that kind of odd."

"Some would call it being attuned to you." He shrugged.

"But I don't mind odd, so long as you're smiling when you say it."

She sobered and let him see her earnest sincerity. "No one has cared whether or not I smiled before, and certainly not if I dreamed. You do." The certainty in that rested tenderly on her shoulders. "I'm grateful for you, Plumber."

"I'm grateful for you, too, Gabby." He touched a hand to her cheek. "I've waited a long time for you."

She managed a shaky smile. "Thank you for that, too."

He smiled, then stepped back. "We'll work out the details on this later. Right now, we have to go. Pastor Ruther is waiting, and he isn't the most patient man in the world."

She'd noticed and been warned about that. "Just tell me I can afford this place," she said, walking toward the front window, already imagining a table for four there with flowers and a teapot on it. There would always be hot tea at Gabby's Treasures. She could barely contain her excitement.

"Absolutely, you can." He smiled and opened the door.

Reluctant to go, she stepped out onto the sidewalk and looked back. In her mind, she saw a rectangular brass sign on the wall beside the door with Gabby's Treasures etched into it. "This is . . ." She couldn't find the words.

"What?" Plumber locked up then fell into step beside her.

"Overwhelming." Her voice sounded husky, frail. Was it possible for your heart to feel this full?

"When you do what you love in a place you love, and you build a life you love, things have a way of falling into place."

"But it's all so perfect." She stopped on the sidewalk. "Perfect happens to other people. It doesn't happen to me."

"Didn't." He lifted his eyebrows, challenging her. "It does now."

Because of him. "You overwhelm me."

"You matter to me, Gabby." They walked down to the pier.

"You matter to me, too." In the distance, Gabby saw Lys and Sara, pulling a roll of fencing out of the backend of a van with Sara Blossoms written on its side. "I'm late."

"So am I," Plumber said. "But it was worth it. See you in a bit."

"Take some brownies to the guys. It'll put them in a forgiving mood."

"Good idea." He grabbed two tins and took off in a sprint toward a clearing where Pastor Ruther and a small gaggle of men stood talking.

Gabby walked on and spoke to Lys. "Hey, I thought you had a poacher to catch."

"Kelly had an emergency," Lys said. "Some report she has to get done before she can come down here, so I'm helping Sara. Besides, it's almost Christmas."

Gabby passed her a tin of brownies and read between the lines. Lys didn't want to lockup anyone this close to Christmas.

Sara snagged a tin. "Mine, right?"

"Absolutely." Gabby grinned. "I know your sweet tooth is in overdrive all the time."

"I love your brownies. You've got to sell them at Gabby's Treasures." Sara opened the tin and bit into one.

"These are for Kelly. No snitching, Sara." Gabby set Kelly's tin in the open backend of the van. "So, what should I do?"

"First things first." Lys parked a hand on her hip. "You can answer a question everyone in Christmas Cove wants answered."

Sara swatted at her. "You're as subtle as mud, Lys."

"What? I want to know, I ask. And I refuse to be lectured to by a woman with brownie crumbs all down the front of her shirt." Lys dipped her chin. "Gabby doesn't have to answer."

"Answer what?" Gabby asked her.

"Are you and Plumber a thing, or what?" Lys shrugged. "You clearly have known each other a while."

"About five years. Maybe a little longer." It'd been five years and two months. Exactly.

"I told you." Lys turned to Sara.

"But you were in an abusive relationship," Sara said. "I assumed, with your husband."

Gabby's face heated. "I've never been married," she said, refusing to lie to her friends.

"Plumber hasn't either," Lys said. "Which has dismayed many a woman around here, and their mothers."

"I told you a long time ago he was in love with someone from away." Sara's eyes sparkled. "It's been you all along."

Gabby laughed, nervous at being put on the spot. "I don't think so."

"So, you do or do not have a thing?" Lys tugged at a roll of fencing and dropped it to the ground, then leaned it against the van's bumper.

"To be honest, I'm not sure. We care about each other. Beyond that, I don't know."

"They do." Sara looked knowingly at Lys. "Plumber has never brought anyone here before, and he's never gotten serious about anyone for as long as I've known him."

"How long have you known him?" Gabby asked, relieved to hear he wasn't married and this insightful tidbit from Sara.

"His whole life."

"Fair warning," Lys said. "We saw the way he looks at you. He's all in. If you're not serious about him, don't play games."

"I don't play games," Gabby assured her. She did have a thing for Plumber, and unless her instincts were totally off, he had one for her, too. But that was something he'd have to reveal to them when and if he saw fit. "I wouldn't know where to begin playing games."

163

"All right, then." Lys looked beyond Gabby's shoulder. Her expression turned tense. "Uh-oh."

Gabby instinctively turned to see what was wrong.

A flustered Kelly was running down the middle of the street toward them. "Where's Plumber?"

"What's wrong, Kelly?" Lys asked.

"The Chief laid down the law. If I don't get this report uploaded to the system in the next thirty minutes, he's going to fire me. That's what's wrong."

"It's been due for a week."

"I know that, Sara. I've been busy getting the cottage ready."

Gabby had created problems for her. "I'm sorry, Kelly."

"So, if you've got thirty minutes, what are you doing here?" Leave it to Lys to cut through the clutter.

Kelly looked a shade shy of panic. "Something fritzed out in the computer and it keeps eating my report, which is why I need Plumber."

"Oh, boy." Sara, not Lys responded. "He left a few minutes ago, I suspect, headed to Carl's Crossing to pick up building supplies for the podium and stage."

Lys crossed her chest with her arms. "No way he'll be back in thirty minutes."

Kelly let out a wounded animal sound. "What am I going to do?"

"Isn't there anyone else in town who can help?" Gabby asked.

"No." Kelly grumbled her worry. "No one."

This was Gabby's fault. If Kelly hadn't been shopping for her and preparing the cottage, she'd have gotten her report in. Plumber would not approve, but Gabby had no choice. She frowned. "Calm down and tell me. What's the computer doing?"

Kelly lifted a hand. "Eating my bloody report."

"How?" Gabby kept her voice calm. "Walk me through it —and be specific."

"I open the document and the machine freezes up. It won't let me do anything but shut down and start over."

Gabby processed that. "Blue screen?"

"Yes!" Kelly growled. "I hate that blue screen."

"Maybe I can help," Gabby said. "I don't know it all, but I've run into the blue-screen monster before."

"Oh, thank you!" Kelly grabbed Gabby's arm and hauled her down the street and into the police station. "It's right back here."

In a shallow alcove, the computer sat atop a desk that stretched wall-to-wall.

Gabby slid onto the chair's seat and began running diagnostics that were second nature to her. In a matter of minutes, she had vanquished the blue-screen monster and recovered a copy of Kelly's report. She copied and pasted a backup copy of it into a second document, added copy to the title, saved it, and then called out. "Kelly."

Kelly scooted over toward her. "You did it—and got a copy of my report!"

"I've already saved the original and a backup copy. So just go where you need to go to upload it, then copy and paste the copy in, submit, and you'll have it done."

Relief flooded Kelly's face. "Wonderful. Thank you, Gabby. You really did save my job."

"You're welcome." Gabby started to stand.

Hearing footfalls from the street door behind her, Kelly turned and stepped out of the alcove. "Good morning. Can I help you gentlemen with something?"

"I hope so," a man said.

Gabby went board stiff. His voice. *Agent Bain.* He'd found her!

"I'll be right with you." Kelly took one look at Gabby's

face, stepped back into the alcove, then whispered, "What's wrong?"

Gentlemen. More than one. "There are two of them?" Gabby mumbled, horrified. When Kelly nodded, Gabby said, "Describe the second man."

"Tall, bald, mid-fifties, short beard."

"Oh, no." Gabby shot to her feet. "I've got to get out of here. Right now."

Kelly blocked her. "What is it?"

"They're trouble for me, Kelly. Please, please don't tell them I'm here." She grabbed Kelly's sleeve. "Please!"

"I won't. I promise." Kelly positioned her body to block Bain's view of Gabby. "Thanks, Mac. Appreciate the assist." Kelly dropped her voice. "I'll keep them busy in here. You go out the back." She shoved Gabby toward the back door.

Gabby ran down the hallway and out the back door, and she kept running all the way to the dock where Lys and Sara were tacking up a stretch of fencing. "Is Plumber back?"

"He just pulled in," Lys said. "Gabby, wait. You look like you've seen a ghost. You okay?"

"Fine." She took off in a sprint to find Plumber, spotted him at the clearing.

He saw her coming, took one look at her face, and ran to meet her. "What's wrong?"

"Bain is here. He's in the police station right now. And the Medros thug—Bain's partner, who picked up the thumb drives and asked me about Rogan Gregos is with him!"

Plumber's worry manifested on his face. Drawing his mouth down into a flat line, he scanned the street. "We've got to get you out of here." They rushed to the Jeep. "Get in and stay down."

Gabby pulled the door open then shut it behind her and wedged herself between the floorboard and seat. She rested her cheek against the cold leather. Her heart thudded in her ears, threatening to pound out of her chest.

When Plumber got inside, he said, "You're going to be okay. You hear me? You're going to be okay."

Tears she didn't want to shed soaked her face. "I don't want to leave here."

"You won't have to leave." He keyed the engine and took off. "I promise."

"But they're here, Plumber. I can't stay."

"You can. I'll find a way." He pressed a number on his phone—someone on speed-dial. "Hunter," Plumber said, revealing he'd called the troops. "It's SW. You know that photo Gabby IDed? Yeah, that one. I need info right now. Status is critical. He's here—with Bain."

Gabby pulled out her phone. "I should call Justin Wade."

SW went still. "That's not necessary."

Not necessary? "Is Hunter Justin Wade?"

"Not exactly." Plumber's attention shifted. "Yeah, Hunter. Go ahead." He listened and then repeated to Gabby. "Mick Fallon is his name. He really is Rogan Gregos's cousin."

"Who is Rogan Gregos?" Gabby asked.

"Holding her gaze, Plumber told Hunter, "Send me a photo of Rogan Gregos ASAP. It looks like it's total truth time." He paused to listen, then added, "No, she isn't going to take it well, which is why I've been avoiding telling her. But she needs to know now." Another pause. Still holding her gaze, Plumber went on. "I know that, okay? I tell her, and I'm fried. Bottomline, better me than her." Plumber took in a sharp breath. "Just get me the photo, Hunter. Please."

Total truth. He had been lying to her? Fried? What did that mean? "Plumber?" It was warm in the Jeep, yet Gabby felt freezing cold inside. What truth could he possibly tell her that would fry him?

"There's something you need to know. Something you

should know, and I will tell you. But first, I need to put some space between Bain and Fallon and us."

Plumber had been lying to her because she wouldn't take whatever this truth was well. That mysterious *something* he had to tell her, and not her *loving* anything like he'd said, had made him force things fall into place. Plumber had manipulated her. Used her. But for what?

Her heart felt bruised, numb, as if it had broken and she hadn't yet realized it. Had anything between them been real? Anything at all?

CHAPTER SEVENTEEN

Tuesday, December 15, 12:05 p.m.

DREAD LAY HEAVY IN GABBY. Plumber drove back to the cottage, his face grimmer than she'd ever seen it. Whatever this truth that would fry him was, it was huge.

"Let's get inside. It's safer." He got out and walked around the front of the Jeep, scanning the woods beyond the lawn, and then onto the porch.

Gabby joined him and he turned his back to her, continuing to hold watch while she unlocked the door and disarmed the alarm system. Her hand shook so hard, it took her two tries. "Okay."

He came in, closed and locked the door. When he removed his jacket, she saw a weapon in his shoulder holster.

She walked to the bar and sat on the stool, afraid her knees would fold before she got there. *How had they found her? How?*

Plumber walked around the counter and opened the fridge, poured two glasses of iced tea, then pulled out the makings for turkey and swiss sandwiches. She wanted to demand he explain right now. Wanted to, but couldn't make herself do it. So instead, she waited patiently for him to gather his thoughts and break whatever this was to her in his own way.

He grabbed two plates and the loaf of bread, then sliced tomato. "This is hard."

"I can see that." She twisted her hands on her lap.

"Plumber, it's Kelly." Her voice carried into the cottage before her footfalls sounded on the porch. "I'm coming in."

He frowned.

So did Gabby.

The door sprang open and Kelly charged in. Lys and Sara followed her but hung back.

"The FBI?" Kelly shouted. "Special Agent Bain is all over my back, demanding I produce Gabby Blake—which I assume is you." She glared from Plumber to Gabby then back to Plumber. "One of you better start explaining. Right now. He's demanding to know where you are, Gabby. Not asking. Demanding."

Plumber paused slicing the tomatoes. "Want a sandwich?"

"I want answers!" Kelly fumed.

"And I'll explain everything," he said calmly. "But I need a few minutes with Gabby first."

"No," Kelly said. "The Chief is primed to fire me already and now this. You'll explain now." She lifted a hand. "Bain is making threats like I've never heard in my life, and that jerk with him acts like a bald hitman."

Plumber looked his sister right in the eye. "That's because he is."

Gabby grunted. "There was something familiar about him —the first time I saw him, but—" Finally, that niggling piece of the puzzle escaping her floated up from her memory and slid into place. Fallon was one of the two men with the old stranger on the street—clearly a longtime Medros man—who mistook her for Helena. Not the one who spoke to her—*He forgets*, he'd said—the other man.

"Oh, for pity's sake. Look in the mirror, Gabby." Kelly slung the words at her. "You look enough like him to be related."

Her jaw fell slack. "No." *Impossible.*

"Yes!" All three of the triple threat answered at once.

Gabby frowned. *Did she?*

"Enough, Kelly." Plumber gave her a look that said in no uncertain terms to back off. "You have no idea what you're doing here."

Kelly jutted her jaw. "Which is why I am not leaving here without answers."

Sara stepped forward, put a hand on Kelly's arm. "Stop. We're all upset. He'll give you your answers. He already said he would." Plumber's level of upset was intense, and it radiated from him. "Let's go out on the porch for a few minutes."

"Sara's right." Lys stepped forward, snitched the sandwich and glass of tea closest to Plumber. "Make yourself another. I'm starving."

Sara mumbled something softly to Kelly, who suddenly seemed to see through the haze of her anger to Gabby's dread and Plumber's upset. "Okay. We'll give you a few minutes. But you better tell me the truth when I come back, brother dear, and I mean it."

The three exited to the porch.

Plumber pulled two more slices of bread from the loaf and set it on his plate. "We don't have much time."

Gabby agreed. "Kelly is short on patience."

He shoved the untouched sandwich toward Gabby and then began making himself one. "This isn't going to be easy on either of us, but like I told Hunter, you need to know the truth. It's time."

"Okay."

"Bain tracking you here with Mick Fallon makes it imperative you know."

"How did they find me here?"

"Fallon had to have tracked you. Or Bain did. What do you still have that you had with you at your father's the day they came for the thumb drives?"

She thought a long second. "I'm not sure. I left everything behind in the Mustang." She had. Her purse, wallet, keys and phone. She thought back, harder, and the answer hit her. "My coat."

"Let me see it."

Plumber examined the jacket and found what he sought. "One of them put this tracking chip in your coat." He held it for her to see.

"So they knew where I was all along."

"Maybe. But they likely lost you at some point."

"Then how?"

"If they suspected you were still alive, one of their golden boy accountants could have tracked the money." Plumber looked beside himself. "TruthSeeker and I took all kinds of precautions, but the money does end up in Christmas Cove, so . . ."

Thoughtful, Plumber took a bite of his sandwich, chewed and swallowed. "If I could have spared you this, I would have, Gabby. It's important you know that."

"Important how?"

"To me." He went to the pantry and came back with chips. Glanced at her plate. "You aren't eating."

If she tried to swallow right now, she'd choke. "I'm fine."

"Eat."

She took a bite, washed it down with tea. "Why is it important to you? Because of your job?"

"No. Because you are important to me."

The second bite went down a little easier. "I'm not going

to break, Plumber. I'm not that fragile or I wouldn't have survived childhood."

"All right. I'm going to take you at your word." He nodded. "Your mother did not die in childbirth with you."

"What?" Of all he could have said, that Gabby least expected.

"She died hours after you were born . . ."

"Convulsions? Stroke? Or what?"

"Lethal injection," he said. "Given to her under orders from Medros."

Gabby gasped. And the incidental encounter of the old man on the street flickered through her mind again. He'd claimed she looked like his sister's husband, Rogan. She'd been so floored by him calling her Helena, Gabby had forgotten that. He'd told the two men rushing him to the SUV something . . . *I must see George now.* That was it. Had her mother known them? Had the old stranger been talking about George Medros? Fallon, when pretending to be Bain's partner and asking her about Rogan Gregos been sending her a warning, identifying himself as Rogan Gregos at the Handel security breach. But was this Rogan also the same man as the old stranger's brother-in-law she supposedly favored? She'd thought it impossible but with the triple threat's comments and all this, suddenly, it all seemed plausible. "I, um, I think I should call Justin Wade and have him listen in on this."

Regret seeped into Plumber's face and settled in the grooves alongside his mouth. "That isn't necessary."

"I think it is."

"It's not."

"Why not?"

He forced himself to meet her gaze. "Because I am Justin Wade."

She absorbed the shock without falling off the barstool. Honestly, after everything else, this revelation seemed like just one more thing. "Is that your real name, or another moniker you've adopted? You're racking up quite a list of them."

"It's my real name and this is my real life, when I'm not working undercover—which I have been doing for some time.

A truth gobsmacked her. "Shadow Watcher was a cover."

"Yes."

Another truth slammed into her. "I didn't find Troop Search and Rescue, you found me."

"Actually, I replaced the original Shadow Watcher early on. When you made first contact with Troop Search and Rescue."

"Why?"

"Because I was doing my job."

"What exactly is your job?" she asked, reeling. "Does Justin Wade work for the FBI?"

"Indirectly," he admitted. "I'm a security specialist, and my firm does contract work for many government entities. The FBI is one of them."

"What company do you work for?"

"I'll tell you, Gabby, but I'm only allowed to tell one person in my lifetime, so I'm trusting you not to share it."

"I won't."

"I work for Silencers, Inc. As consultants, we do the jobs that are complicated, and others can't do for a multitude of reasons." He wiped his mouth with a napkin. "But I probably won't be employed there much longer."

The fried comment between him and Hunter came to mind, but Gabby didn't dare to assume anything at this point. "Why not?"

"Because what I'm telling you will get me fired."

She frowned. "What exactly are you telling me, Plumber?"

He washed down his tea, then refilled his glass from the

pitcher. "It started when your father was a little boy. He had a good life back then. But he was friends with a kid in his neighborhood who wasn't so lucky. His friend didn't have the best parents and he had none of the opportunities your dad did. No educational chances—all that goes with rough parenting. That made him vulnerable, and your father knew it. So, he became the guy's best friend. Your father had a devoted streak a mile wide, Gabby."

"I had no idea of any of this."

"I know."

"Who was the boy he befriended?"

"Rogan Gregos."

So the old man on the street had been mistaken about her, but he had associated her father and Rogan. Which did nothing to explain why Gabby and Rogan physically favored.

"Rogan Gregos was easy prey for Medros. He's famous for exploiting vulnerable kids like Rogan. Medros has a daughter named Mia. She fell in love with Rogan. And Rogan saw marriage to Mia as his one shot for a better life. George Medros opposed; he wanted better for his daughter, but Mia insisted. So, Rogan married her, and they had two children."

Gabby had a bad feeling about this. A terrible feeling. Her hand to her chest, she cringed. "Tell me I'm not one of their children."

"No, you're not."

Plumber's words should have been reassuring, but for some unspoken and as yet unexplained reason, they weren't. Gabby intuitively held her breath, waiting for the other shoe to drop.

"That's where my firm came in. Actually," he rubbed his chin. "It was a similar firm, owned by the father of the man who owns my firm. The father's company was tasked with an infiltration operation inside Medros's organization. The father's company sent an operative in undercover. A female operative." Plumber paused to give Gabby time to absorb that. "Rogan Gregos took one look at her and fell in love."

"His daughter marrying a man he didn't approve of, now in love with another woman." Gabby said. "Not promising conditions for Rogan's prospects of a long and healthy life." Medros killed people left and right. Dishonoring his daughter? Only a fool would deliberately antagonize Medros like that. But love made fools of people...

Plumber gauged Gabby's reaction, and then went on. "The operative sought Rogan's confidence to gain the information she was after. But that wasn't enough for Rogan. He tried luring her to him, charming her, but she wasn't interested. She was a professional through and through. Everything I've found in her old files and reports was positive. Ethical and principled. A woman everyone seemed to admire."

"So what happened to her?" Gabby asked.

Plumber's face went blank. "Rogan Gregos raped her."

Gabby rebelled. "No!"

"I'm afraid so," Plumber said. "And a child was conceived."

The truth rammed into Gabby and stole her breath. She gasped. "My mother? Helena? She was the operative . . . and the child conceived is me?"

"Yes." Sorrow flooded Plumber's eyes, softened his voice. "Rogan's cousin by marriage, Mick Fallon, agreed to keep Rogan's secret about the rape and the pregnancy, but he didn't."

"Blood is thicker than water."

"True in this case." Plumber looked down at his hands. "Fallon is the son of Mia's brother. He went to his Aunt Mia and told her, hoping for her protection. She was still crazy in love with Rogan, so that wasn't a bad plan. Fallon and Rogan were close, and Fallon was terrified Medros would find out about the baby and kill Rogan for shaming his daughter."

Gabby fought to stay controlled. Conceived in a rape? How could she ever wrap her mind around that, much less her heart? "It didn't work, did it? The plan failed."

"No, it didn't work," Plumber said. "Mia went off the deep end, ran straight to her father and told him everything. Honestly, Mia hasn't been right since then."

Gabby didn't know whether to cry or fly off in a rage. So many conflicting emotions swam through her that she couldn't sort them all. She opened her mouth to speak but her words made no sound. Swallowing hard, she took a second. *Stuff it down. Suck it up and stuff it down.* Then, she made another attempt. "What you're telling me is Rogan Gregos is my real father."

"He is, or was, yes. Medros reacted to Mia's revelation as expected, and . . . Well, Rogan is long since dead."

"How long?"

"Since your mother's pregnancy became obvious." Giving Gabby a minute, Plumber rinsed his plate at the sink. "Medros vowed Rogan would never see his child, and he didn't."

Gabby reached for the chilled glass of tea. Her throat had gone bone dry. She took in a long drink, then set the glass down, pretending she hadn't noticed her hand shaking so badly she nearly dropped the glass onto the counter. "If Rogan Gregos is my father, how did I end up with Adian Blake?"

"Rogan knew Medros would kill him, so he went to his old friend Adian Blake and begged him to marry Helena and take care of her and you. Adian came up with the idea of convincing Medros that Helena was carrying his child, not Rogan's. None of them were happy with the plan, but it was the only possibility for saving Rogan's life and possibly Helena's."

Gabby swallowed hard. "They planned to convince

Medros that Helena was in love with Adian Blake and he and Rogan were lifelong friends." Indignation swelled in Gabby. "The man raped her. Why would my mother agree to that? Why wouldn't Medros just kill her, too, before I was born?"

"Those were different times. A single mom back then was socially problematic, and you personally know how long Medros's reach is. They either worked together or none of them had a chance, including your mother. It was widely known that Medros had a soft spot for babies. If they could all stay alive until Medros saw you, they believed he wouldn't kill any of them."

"Obviously that deduction was flawed."

"Actually, the plan almost worked. It failed because Medros saw the way Rogan looked at your mother. He heard how his voice softened on saying her name. So, Medros didn't believe the story about Helena and Adian, though by then, they were already married."

"Mia was still not herself . . ."

"Exactly." Plumber nodded. "Rogan was to blame for that, and he had to die for it. So Medros ordered the hit, it was executed, and it seemed that satisfied Medros.

"Until he murdered my mother."

Plumber put the sandwich makings back in the fridge. "Until then, yes. You were born and Medros came to the hospital to see you. He obtained proof you were Rogan's child. When he had it, he warned your father—Adian Blake— that Mia was never to see you or him. If she so much as glimpsed either of you, Medros would kill you both. And if you ever so much as mentioned looking for Rogan's family, Medros would kill you both. Mia, Medros insisted, had suffered enough."

"The old man in the street who mistook me for Helena . . ."

"Mia's brother," Plumber said.

"He told Medros he'd seen me."

"We think so, but we don't know that for fact."

"I do." She leaned over the bar. "He told the men getting him into the car that he must see George now. He meant George Medros. I'm certain of it."

"You're likely right."

She took in a sharp, staggered breath. "That's what all this with Medros is about. Not the information on the thumb drives."

"I expect it was both this and the information on the thumb drives."

"But why would my father—Adian Blake—work for Medros?" She shook her head. "That doesn't make sense."

"He was forced into early retirement. He told Medros he needed work to keep up the façade. Medros gave him work that leveraged your father even more. He already had him leveraged with threats on both your lives."

Gabby absorbed and struggled to process it all. "So Adian Blake treated me like a stranger my whole life not because of my mother but because of Medros and his threats?"

"I believe he was trying to protect you. For his friend. His only friend." Plumber stowed the chips back in the pantry. "He couldn't share what he didn't know, and neither could you. I think that's why he made sure you both kept your distance and Rogan Gregos was never mentioned—to stay safe. That said, I also think Adian Blake came to love you, Gabby."

"No, he didn't." She flatly denied it and knew she was right about this. "He didn't know me, and he kept Aunt Janelle from me. She knew the truth. She knew too much, and said so in her letter."

"Janelle terrified your father. He feared she would get you both killed, and herself, too. That's why he kept her away."

That made sense, and Gabby couldn't deny it. "He didn't

know or love me, but he did sacrifice a lot to protect me. He had no joy in his life." She thought about that. "Honestly, he had little life in his life—his job was about it. Whether he did what he did for Rogan, my mother or for me, who knows? I'm betting on Rogan or her. But he did sacrifice to take care of me after they were gone." Her throat thick, Gabby struggled to stay composed. She could deal with the emotions later. Right now, she needed to focus on all he could have had in his own life and hadn't because he'd chosen to continue to protect her. Oh, he protected himself, too, but he had protected her. She owed him for that.

Still, her heart hurt, and her mind tumbled back through the years, through all the isolation and loneliness, through all that hadn't been. She stiffened, knowing that was a bad place to go that could bring nothing good. He hadn't abandoned her. Why he hadn't just left there, she had no idea. Probably his work. Forced retirement had shattered the one thing in his world that was his own, freely chosen and not assumed out of duty to a friend. His work definitely mattered to Adian Blake. And Gabby couldn't resent it or him for that. Considering all he'd forfeited, she just couldn't hold it against him. "I, um, I need a drink of water."

"I'll get it." Plumber stood up. "You stay seated. You've had a lot of shocks here."

She felt numb. Head to toe numb and bruised and sad and somewhere deep inside, a spark of something else. Relief? It felt like relief. Finally, she had answers to questions she'd wondered about most of her life. "I'm fine."

"You're not fine. No one could hear all this and be fine, Gabby." He placed the glass in front of her.

Looking up, she met and held his gaze. "No, I'm not fine."

"Give yourself time."

She lifted the glass and drank, slowly working through all these shocking revelations. Her father not being her father didn't surprise her. He hadn't loved her, but he had come to love Helena . . . or had he?

Gabby would never know. Just as she would never know why Medros let her mother live until Gabby was born and then had her killed. Maybe because, being raped, he'd seen her as a victim, too? Seen Gabby as a source of potential leverage over Rogan? And what about Plumber? Had he sought Gabby out? Of course, he had. But why? She took a page from Lys and just asked the question. "Why did you seek me out?"

Justin wiped down the countertop. "After what happened to your mom, the owner of the firm who had given her the assignment shut down his business."

"The father of your boss at Silencers, right?"

Plumber nodded. "His son grew up and started Silencers. I took over your case five years ago. When you approached Troop Search and Rescue, we had a way in. I became Shadow Watcher."

"You were spying on me."

"Yes."

A sense of betrayal so deep she couldn't define where it started inside her, ran deep and wide and seemed to have no end. Then came the pain. And trust withered and died.

CHAPTER EIGHTEEN

Tuesday, December 15, 12:45 p.m.

"I WAS SPYING ON YOU, yes—but not really," Plumber said. "At least, not in the way you might think."

Trying to retain her very shaky composure, Gabby searched for her voice. "In what way, then?"

"Looking for anything to tell us whether or not you knew the truth—you didn't—and then to keep you from meeting the same fate your mother met."

Gabby believed him. "Why?" She lifted her hands. "Why did you care?"

"Your mother was one of us, Gabby. She was an operative."

Surprise rippled through her. "My father," she started, stopped short and corrected herself. "Adian Blake didn't know that."

"No, he didn't. At least, according to Helena."

"She didn't tell her one person. Not even the man who married her?" What kind of woman did that?

"She told no one. She swore it," Plumber said. "When my

boss's father shut down his firm, he devoted himself to watching over you."

"How long did he do that?"

"Your whole life. When his health failed, his son had already started Silencers, Inc. He promised his father he would continue to watch over you, and he has. They're good people, Gabby."

For all the years she'd felt totally alone, she never had truly been alone. "Because she was one of you, and you lost her." Gabby nodded. "I can see that." She returned her gaze to Plumber. "Your helping me wasn't for me, or because I fascinated you." It sounded silly now. And she felt silly for having believed him. "It was just your job."

"It was my job, that's true." He swiped his knees with his palms. "But I would have watched you with or without Silencers. You truly did fascinate me, Gabby. You still do." Clearly picking up on her skepticism, he let out little noise from the back of his throat. "You have no idea how special you are." He shook his head. "Your mind is sharp and quick, and it's amazing the way you attune to the Troops, warning me when one of them needs attention. No one misses that you genuinely care about them or the kids, as if each missing one is your child." The edges of his mouth curved. "It's always personal for you."

"They're lost and afraid. I know the feeling, and I don't want anyone else going through that."

"I'm sorry you grew up feeling that way. Really sorry." Regret burned in his eyes. "If you knew how many times I thought about just knocking on your door and telling you the truth . . ."

Their one-person rule, which kept them from being recused from cases. "But you couldn't do that."

"Ethically, no, I couldn't." The regret seeped into his tone.

"But I wanted to—and if I had known how it would be between us, I would have."

He had told her now. And as odd as it might sound, she wasn't upset with him or his boss for making her an assignment. It was comforting to know that even when she thought she'd been alone, she hadn't been. That their reason was to honor her mother and not her didn't matter. Someone had been there, watching over her. "For your job?" she pushed, not wanting to read more into this than there was, especially with the all bombshells being dropped.

"No." He stood up. "Well, yes, for my job. But as I got to know you everything changed." He touched her hand. "Gabby, I couldn't believe I'd finally found you."

That confused her. "But I wasn't lost. You, or someone at Silencers, Inc., knew where I was all the time."

"That was the problem. I wasn't free to meet you, to make it personal."

Her heart fluttered. "But . . ."

"But what?"

She had a choice to make. She could accept the reality of the situation or deny it. But if she did deny it, the person who would lose most was her. And Plumber. "But it always has been personal."

He smiled. "I didn't know that until I came here," he reminded her.

She rubbed his thumb with the pad of her finger. "True."

"It's always been personal for me, Gabby."

"Always?" What did he mean?

"I went through the 'I'm being crazy' and 'it's impossible' phases, but I knew better. Two years ago, I went into my boss to quit. I told him I'd fallen in love and I couldn't do anything about that so long as I worked there. When I told him about the woman, he reminded me I had signed an NDA and he threatened to enforce it."

She'd signed a non-disclosure agreement at Handel. "Could he enforce it?"

"They don't hold up in most states," Plumber admitted. "But he did make a threat he could enforce, and it would cost me huge."

"What did he threaten?"

"He'd get my security clearance revoked."

"He really could do that?"

"Oh, yeah. And if he did, that would blackball me in the field. I'd never be able to work for anyone, doing what I do, without clearance."

Obviously, Plumber had forfeited the woman. He was still working for Silencers. "Who was she?"

Standing facing each other, Plumber clasped both of her hands in his. "The woman was you, Gabby."

"Really?" She wanted to believe him. Every instinct in her body swore she could believe him.

"Really. I knew it the first time I saw you."

That surprised her. "You saw me before coming here?" When he nodded, she asked, "Where?"

On Rue de Royale."

She only went one place on Rue de Royale. "At the scent shoppe?"

That faraway look lighted his eyes. "You were inside, sniffing the scents. I was outside, looking in through the window, and you got this look. I love that look, and I'll never forget it."

"What kind of look?"

He held her gaze. "Captivated."

Her face heated. "I love scents."

"I knew right then no other woman would do. It had to be you."

The door swung open and Kelly barged in. "Okay, Plumber, tell her you love her already. We waited through the shockers—" she paused and looked at Gabby "—Sorry about your dad . . . and about your mom."

"Yeah, we are." Lys shrugged. "But man, Adian Blake was some kind of devoted, wasn't he?"

"I respect that." Sara told Lys, then cut her glance to Gabby. "For what it's worth, I agree with Plumber. Adian loved you. He was scared to know anything because him knowing anything could get you killed."

Kelly cut in. "Later. I've been patient long enough. It's cold out there."

"Then you heard I was Plumber's assignment," Gabby said. "He doesn't love me. So, don't push him into saying something he doesn't mean."

"If you don't mind," Plumber interjected, and stared at Gabby. "He does love you. I love you. I have for a long time."

"Okay, then," Lys said. "Never thought you'd get there, Plumber, but glad you did. And I'm calling it settled." She clapped her hands together. "Now can we please focus on what are we going to do to keep Bain and Mick Fallon from killing Gabby?"

Sara frowned. "We need a plan."

"We do." Kelly looked from Plumber to Gabby and then to Sara. "A really good one." She hugged Gabby. "I'm really am sorry about your parents."

He loved her. Gabby had never expected to hear those words from anyone, much less from a man like Plumber. Or in a situation like this. Still, her heart might be bruised and battered, but love was in it, too. He loved her.

Plumber stepped back, spoke to Gabby. "I know you are floored and angry, and you can't forgive me for not telling you the truth sooner—"

"No one could forgive that, brother dear," Kelly said.

"You're not helping," Plumber chastised his sister.

"Sorry."

"I know you can't forgive me yet," he went on. "But I am asking you to, and I am asking you to trust me."

Forgive and trust him? Now? Hard. Really hard. But after all he had done to protect her. To get her to safety. To help her. "Trust you with what?" Gabby asked.

"I have a plan," he said. His expression sobered. "Fair warning. If it fails, we'll likely both die."

Gabby frowned. "That's not reassuring, Plumber."

"No, but it's the truth," he shot back at her. "And if it works, you can really live."

"Life's a risk. It's a shot at all she wants," Kelly grumbled. "Let's hear it."

He looked at his sister. "I'll need your help. It's dangerous. But with Bain and Fallon already here, there's no time to get an operative in to do it—and not a word out of any of you about my job or my company or I'll cut your tongues out." He narrowed his gaze. "I am not exaggerating."

"We heard. One person only," Lys said. "Which is why we have no idea what you're talking about."

"Right." Sara agreed.

Kelly nodded. "You fix computers."

They stood firm with him. Gabby loved that. "I don't want Kelly in danger because of me, Plumber. Whatever you need done, can't I do it?"

"No, I'm afraid not," he said then went on to explain. "Kelly is a trained law enforcement officer. Our odds for success are better with her, Gabby. But you'll have to pretend to be her while she's pretending to be you."

Kelly stiffened. "I can't do that. Bain talked to me at the station. He knows me."

"I'll do it," Lys said. "He doesn't know me, and I'm trained."

"Lys, if I were lost in the woods, you'd be the one I'd pray would be searching for me. But I need Kelly for this. She reads me well. Always has. We could need that edge."

"He's right about that, Lys." Sara pointed heavenward with a fingertip. "I can think of at least a dozen occasions over the years—"

"All right." Lys glared at Sara.

Plumber pivoted to his sister. "We'll disguise you. No one will recognize you."

"If she's going to be disguised, I can be disguised," Gabby insisted. "I told you, I don't want Kelly at risk, too."

"You can't shoot," he said. "She can. If the need arises, I need backup."

Gabby took in a sharp breath.

Plumber ignored it. "Gabby, you're going to be dressed as a cop. Kelly will get you a uniform."

"This isn't going to work, Plumber," Sara said.

"It will work. It has to work. If it doesn't, those men are going to kill Gabby and I'm going to have to kill them."

Kelly took that in. "We'll make it work. Just don't shoot up Christmas Cove, Plumber, and I mean it."

She turned to Lys and Sara. "You spread the word and get us some help out here. Tell everyone exactly what's at stake, and that Gabby needs our help. Pastor Ruther will activate the call list. Go to him first."

Plumber passed the chip he'd removed from Gabby's coat. "Plant this on a truck leaving town."

"Tracked her here, huh?" Lys frowned. "On it." Lys moved toward the door.

"Don't worry, Gabby. We won't let you down." Sara walked out and closed the door.

"Kelly, stop them. I can't ask the people here to put themselves at risk. I just can't."

"They won't ask," Kelly assured her. "I'm serious. People

in Christmas Cove—all of us protect each other. The only thing Sara and Lys have to say is Gabby's in trouble."

"That's not true." Gabby didn't believe her. "No one does that for someone they never met, or that they barely know." Gabby's gaze slid to Plumber. "People just aren't built that way."

"They are here, Gabby," Plumber said. "You've made some friends already. I was at the coffee shop and Alyce Crawley told me about the chest you gave her daughter. You wanted it for your store, she said, but you knew her daughter loved that chest and she'd been eyeing it for months."

"The clerk told me."

"You bought it and gifted it to her."

"I wanted her to have something she loved for Christmas."

"Alyce won't forget that."

"I didn't do it to be remembered," Gabby said, explaining herself.

"I know. So did Alyce." He tilted his head. "Then you asked her if she had a problem with you selling exotic teas?"

"She owns the coffeeshop."

"It was considerate."

"She told me, too." Kelly chimed in. "She was touched by that. So were the other vendors. "I'm going to go pick up a uniform for Gabby and some disguise props. Be back shortly."

When Kelly left, Gabby turned to Plumber. "So, Alyce told you about the chest and the tea?"

Plumber nodded. "But I already knew about the chest. Pastor Ruther told me, and he said you were exactly the kind of role model others needed. A good example for the likes of me."

Gabby gasped. "You're a wonderful role model."

"I'll tell him you said so. He's remembering too many incidents from my early years." Plumber disappeared upstairs for a second and returned with a duffle bag. He set it down, unzipped it, and began pulling out guns.

"Ah, I see." Gabby tried not to overreact. She paced a few steps toward the French door, then turned. "I get that Kelly and I are to pose as each other. But what does that do for us? I'm not getting the big picture on your plan."

"Bain is looking for Gabby Johnson." His hands full, Plumber moved place to place—a bookshelf, a cabinet, the microwave. "So, we're going to have him meet Gabby Johnson . . ."

Why was he stashing weapons all over the cottage? Anxiety rose in her. "You're going to bring Bain and Fallon *here?*"

Near the fridge, Plumber stopped and looked over at her. A wicked twinkle lit in his eyes. "What better way to convince them you're not their Gabby Johnson?"

"Oh, I don't know about this." Gabby wasn't sold on this plan. Not at all sold on it, and she didn't think bringing Bain and Fallon to this cottage—*to her home*—was a safe move. "It seems unnecessarily risky to me."

"It is risky. But we don't have a lot of options."

Minutes later, he walked from the kitchen back over to her. "Kelly's coming up the drive right now. You're going to need to put on the uniform and go to the police station, then stay put there until I come for you."

"Coming in," Kelly called out from the porch. The door cracked open and a woman walked in who looked nothing like Kelly. Her hair was red, her face totally devoid of makeup, and she was dressed in coveralls and a t-shirt mostly hidden by an unbuttoned white shirt that hung almost to her knees. But the most shocking thing was the dark-haired toddler resting on her hip, smiling up at her and calling her mama.

"Kelly?"

"Gabby Johnson," she said. "My son, Jeremy."

Gabby got gooseflesh. "Whose child is that?"

"Alyce's grandson," Kelly said. "She figured he'd lower the odds of any gunplay—and he calls everyone Mama."

Kelly smiled—and had totally different looking teeth. For the first time, Gabby's uncertainty about Plumber's plan fell to an infusion of hope that it actually would work. She looked at him. "Bain will never identify her as Kelly Meyer."

"Counting on that. Get into the uniform."

In short order, Gabby emerged from the bedroom in uniform with her hair tucked up under the hat, her expression stern. "This isn't going to fool anybody."

"It doesn't have to," Plumber said. "The uniform will keep them away from you."

They'd walked right into the police station earlier, but they hadn't been there then to commit murder, so he was probably right.

"It's time for you to go." He guided Gabby to the door. "Remember. Go straight to the station and stay put until I come and get you."

That still didn't sit right with her. They were taking all the risks. She opened her mouth to object.

His hand on her cheek stopped her. "I know. It'll be fine."

If it would be fine, then why had he stashed weapons all over the cottage? She thought it, but held her tongue, stretched on her toes and kissed him. "Be careful."

"We will."

Gabby prayed he was right. If anything happened to any of them—*a child!*—she'd never survive the guilt. Never.

"We'll be fine," Kelly waved.

"You better," Gabby said, trembling, her eyes burning. "I've only had three friends in my life and one Plumber." She blinked hard. "I can't lose anything else. I just . . . can't."

"Have faith, Gabby." Plumber ushered her the rest of the way to the door, and the second she stepped onto the porch, he pushed it shut.

"Weapons in the usual places?" Kelly's voice carried out onto the porch.

"Yeah. We're good."

"Okay, then. Bain and Fallon will be here at five o'clock . . .."

CHAPTER NINETEEN

Tuesday, December 15, 4:15 p.m.

TECHNICALLY, Gabby kept her word. She went straight to the station. But then she made a U-turn in the parking lot and drove down Main Street. She could not sit sheltered in the safety of the station while Plumber and Kelly and little Jeremy took all the risks for her. She had to go back. She'd hide in the woods nearby, then if trouble erupted, she could at least intervene as a distraction.

To do it effectively, she needed a weapon she could just aim and fire. She'd never before held a gun much less fired one, but Bain didn't know that, and to protect Plumber or Kelly or little Jeremy, Gabby would do it.

At the curb, she pulled to a stop in front of Alyce's coffeeshop. It was dark inside and the sign on the door read: *Closed*.

Finding that strange, Gabby looked down Main Street. Everything was closed—all the shops. Pulling out her phone, she dialed Sara. Her call went straight to voice mail. So did

Lys's. As a last resort, Gabby called Pastor Ruther. "Voice mail." Where was everybody?

The station would have weapons. But they weren't apt to let Gabby waltz in and appropriate one. Kelly was off the chief's hit list for firing since Gabby helped her get the computer fixed and her report uploaded, but Gabby borrowing a weapon would certainly get Kelly right back on it and demoted or fired. That the triple threat had adopted her as a fourth in their group was known all over Christmas Cove.

At Patchwork Needle, Gabby spotted something leaning against the bench Leigh Pace had sitting out front near the door. Gabby stopped. A baseball bat. "Well, it's better than nothing."

She retrieved the bat and then headed back toward the cottage. How odd Main Street seemed with absolutely no one around. She'd never seen it deserted, regardless of the day or time she'd driven in. Another festival workday? Something significant had to be going on. Strange that Kelly hadn't mentioned anything.

About a mile from the mailbox and turn, Gabby pulled off the road and into the woods, hiding the Malibu from view behind dense foliage. Grabbing the bat, she took off toward the cottage, avoiding the driveway and getting too close to the clearing.

The branches underfoot crunched with her steps. In the silent woods, the sound seemed magnified. To her left, something scurried off. She glimpsed it from the corner of her eye but couldn't make out what she'd seen. Probably a raccoon or something like that. Trying hard to move soundlessly, she gave up on that. The undergrowth was too brittle and dry, so she hoped for making minimal noise instead.

Curving around trees in her path, she made her way to a point lining up with the far end of the front porch, hoping Bain and Fallon would park close enough that, should the need arise, she could get to them before they got to Plumber or Kelly.

In position behind a massive twisted oak, Gabby checked her watch. Five o'clock. Her heart raced, and she touched a hand to her chest. *Please, keep them safe. Please. Please . . .*

A car approached on the driveway. It was black. As it drew closer, she recognized it as an SUV, so seeing Fallon behind the wheel didn't surprise her. The door to the cottage opened and Plumber and Kelly stepped out onto the porch. Jeremy, parked on Kelly's hip, wailed at the top of his lungs. That did surprise Gabby. The child had a sunny disposition and had been all smiles and giggles. Now he raged, and he definitely had a set of lungs on him. Trying to calm him down, Kelly ducked back into the cottage and then came right back out onto the porch. She'd wrapped a blanket around Jeremy and held him snuggled to her chest. It didn't seem to slow his crying. If anything, it intensified.

Fallon and Bain got out of the SUV. "Hello. I'm Agent Bain, FBI." He looked around and raised his voice to be heard over Jeremy. "Officer Meyer was supposed to be here."

"She called," Plumber said. "There's been an accident at the festival. She's been delayed. She said she was going to call you and postpone, but we told her your coming without her was fine. We'd talk to you on our own. Must be important to bring you all the way out here." Plumber walked closer to the edge of the porch. "So, what can we do for you, Agent Bain?"

Kelly stepped forward. "I'm so sorry about the crying. I can see you cringing from here. He's teething, poor angel. It's a nightmare."

Bain feigned a sympathetic nod. "Are you Gabby Johnson?"

"I am, though at the moment, I half-wish I was anyone else."

Bain actually smiled. "I remember those days."

"Tell me they end."

"Afraid not." He grunted. "You just go from worrying about one thing to another until they're about twenty-five. Doesn't stop then, but you do get breaks now and then."

"I was afraid of that." Kelly grunted, bounced the baby at her chest. "Well, at least there are good moments, too."

As if on cue, Jeremy started screaming, "Mama. Mama. Cookie, Mama."

"In a minute, honey." She smiled at him, and he started wailing again. "I am so sorry," she told Fallon and Bain in a voice strange to Gabby's ears.

"It's not her," Fallon told Bain. "Let's go."

Bain nodded. "We're sorry to have troubled you," he said. Our Ms. Johnson has been missing. Her family is deeply concerned. We've been searching for her, and we'd hoped we'd found her here, but clearly we have not."

"No trouble," Plumber said.

"Why would anyone show up here that doesn't have to be here?" Kelly asked, making it clear she wasn't a fan of Christmas Cove.

"We don't know that she would," Bain said. "We got a tip she could be here, and so we had to check it out. If a stranger comes around with your same name, will you let us know right away?" Bain passed Plumber a business card. "You can reach me on the mobile twenty-four seven."

Plumber took the card. "Do we need to be careful, Agent? Is your Gabby Johnson dangerous?"

"Oh, no. No."

Plumber feigned confusion. "Then why are you looking for her?"

"We're trying to find her to protect her."

"From what?" he pushed.

"I'm afraid I can't divulge that information," Bain said. His regret almost sounded genuine.

"Well, I hope you're successful," Kelly said. "I can't see anyone coming here on purpose, but if she should, it's good to know she's not a serial killer or something."

"My wife bends a little low on the dramatic side," Plumber lowered his voice. "Is there any reason that whatever you're trying to protect your Ms. Johnson from will impact my wife? Her having the same name brought you here. Could it bring—"

"No, not to worry. There's no way your wife could be mistaken for Gabby Johnson. The other Gabby Johnson, I mean."

Plumber looked a little affronted and sniffed. "If we hear of anything, we'll let you know." He looked at Kelly. Take the baby inside. It's cold out here, and his wailing is rattling my nerves."

"Sorry, honey." Kelly went into the cottage and closed the door.

Plumber looked back at Bain. "I'm recalling fondly my days of—"

"Solitude?"

"Peace and quiet," Plumber said. "But I could settle for solitude."

Fallon was on the phone. "Got it." He turned toward the SUV. "We need to move. They just picked up a signal about twenty miles south of here."

Bain stared long and hard at Plumber.

He didn't flinch. "Have a good day, Agent Bain—and Merry Christmas."

"Merry Christmas." He pivoted and he and Fallon hustled back to the SUV.

Plumber stayed on the porch and watched until Bain and Fallon cleared the driveway and turned onto the paved road.

Gabby forced herself not to rush to the porch, to stay put

in the woods. She even entertained the idea of speeding back to the station, but the deception in that galled her.

"Gabby?" Plumber called out. "You can come out now."

She gulped in a sharp breath. He knew she was here? How had he known?

"Gabby?" He shouted again. "Come out. It's okay."

She cut through the trees to the porch and climbed the steps.

"Did you even go to the station?" Plumber was vexed, and she couldn't really blame him. "Well, did you?"

"I did. But I thought you might need some backup, so I came back."

"With a baseball bat."

"Everything was closed. I couldn't get to a gun." She walked into his arms. "I thought, if push came to shove, I could be a distraction."

"And grateful we are that you couldn't." Kelly came out of the cottage without Jeremy. "People not trained to handle firearms just shouldn't handle firearms."

Gabby hugged her. "I'm glad you're okay." She pulled back. "Where is Jeremy?"

"With Alyce."

"He was right here," Gabby said.

"He was earlier," Kelly said. "He left right after Bain arrived."

"But I saw him in your arms. I heard him crying."

"A recording," Plumber said. "You never saw his face."

That was true. He'd had his head buried against Kelly's shoulder and under the blanket the whole time, and he was wailing so loud, all Gabby had focused on was the crying, him asking for a cookie and crying some more. "I didn't."

Plumber frowned. "In five years, have you ever known me to put a child in jeopardy?"

She hadn't. "Sorry." Gabby should have thought of that. "Kelly, I didn't even recognize your voice."

"That was the objective." She smiled with the strange teeth.

"Thank you for doing this," Gabby said, then looked at Plumber. "And you." She stiffened. "Do you think they'll stay away now?"

"There's no reason for them to come back. This Gabby Johnson is not their Gabby Johnson. She can't be here and twenty miles south at the same time, can she?"

"No, she can't." Gabby smiled. "And she isn't their Gabby Johnson. She's barely even their Gabby Blake anymore."

Plumber frowned. "What do you mean?"

"It's nothing." She shook her head.

"Tell me," he insisted.

"I used to dream of a life like this. One where I could just be me and be happy. One where I knew people's names and they knew mine, and we—"

"We what?" Plumber pushed her to go on.

"We shared our lives. The good and bad, the ups and down. I dreamed about having that kind of life. I prayed for it and wanted it so badly. But down deep I never believed I would actually have it."

"You've got us, Gabby." A woman's voice sounded from behind her on the lawn.

Gabby spun toward the sound and watched the woods come to life with the faces of those she'd already met in Christmas Cove as well as those she hadn't. Lys and Sara walked among them. And they were all armed.

"You're all here for me?" Gabby couldn't believe her eyes. Were they angry with her? She cast a sideward glance at Plumber. "Do they want me to leave?"

"No, they're here to protect you—and Kelly and me." Plumber smiled. "Our backup."

Gabby's jaw fell slack. "I—I can't believe this."

"You're one of us now, Gabby." Plumber hooked an arm around her shoulder. "I told you Lys and Sara wouldn't have to ask for help."

Alyce came forward and hugged Gabby. "You okay, hon?"

"I'm better than I've been in my whole life." She smiled at the group of locals. "Thank you—all of you."

Alyce sniffed. "Those two reeked of trouble. Good riddance to bad rubbish, I say."

Pastor Ruther stepped forward. "The rubbish just checked out of the B & B. Fred is following them to the Interstate to make sure they're gone."

"Thank you." Gabby smiled. "I guess this explains why Main Street was deserted. You're all here."

A collective chuckle rippled to her. "So, it does," the pastor said, then looked at Plumber. "We're headed to the festival, then. Blessing of the Fleet is in an hour. Don't be late!"

"But we already did that." Gabby was confused.

"That was the rehearsal for the locals. This one is the real deal." Pastor stepped forward, touched her hand. "You've had quite the day, Gabby."

She had.

"Don't you worry. You'll be fine. Better than fine. You'll be safe here. This is your home now."

His words filled her empty heart. She'd rarely in her life felt safe or at home. Her throat thick, she whispered, "Thank you, Pastor Ruther."

He nodded then turned. "Everyone, stow your weapons and get to the festival before the funnel cake batter is wrecked." He whispered to Gabby. "That batter goes bad and I'll be in the doghouse for a week."

"Gabby's Treasures isn't ready to open yet, but if you get

into a fix, call me. I'll make you some soaps. They shorten doghouse time."

"Good thinking." He smiled. "Thank you, Gabby."

Plumber and Gabby stood on the porch and watched the cluster of Covers make their way to the main road. A bright yellow school bus pulled to a stop and they all got inside.

"The school bus?" Gabby smiled.

"A string of cars would've stuck out like a sore thumb. Bain would have spotted that."

"True." Gabby grunted, watching the bus pull away. She swiveled to look at Plumber. "Your plan was a lot more developed than I thought."

Kelly emerged from the cottage looking like herself again. "I'll see you two when you get to the festival."

"Thanks again, Kelly," Gabby said.

"No problem. That's what cops and friends do." Kelly made her way down the steps and to her car, then paused at its door and looked back at Gabby. "You're relieved of duty tonight. You've had a wicked day. But next year, I get double-time."

"You got it."

Lys stepped over and hugged Gabby. "Glad you're safe, and I hope this ends the drama."

"Me, too."

"But if it doesn't, we're here. Don't forget that."

"I won't, Lys. Thanks."

"Move it, Sara," Lys said. "I've got a bone to pick with the mayor."

Sara gave Gabby a quick hug, then rushed after Lys. "Lys Hayden, if you put him in a foul mood, Mama and I are going to be really ticked off at you."

Gabby looked at Plumber. "Sara's dad is the mayor?"

Plumber nodded. "Why didn't you stay at the station?"

"You know why."

"Gabby—"

She ignored the warning in his tone. "It worked out fine." Before he could fuss anymore, she kissed him. "I love you, Shadow Watcher, Plumber, Justin Wade."

"Not yet," he said. "You love Shadow Watcher. Maybe even Plumber. But not yet Justin Wade."

"You could be right," she said.

"I am."

"But I do know my own mind, and you could be wrong. Maybe I fell in love with all of you before I ever saw you."

He studied her face and a little twinkle lit in his eye. "Maybe you did."

She smiled.

"So, you forgive me then—for not telling you the truth sooner?"

"I thank you, Plumber. For everything, including loving me. Just so you know, I'm a novice at loving and definitely at being loved. You'll need to bear with me while I learn the ropes."

His expression turned tender. "We'll muddle through it together."

"Promise?"

"I do."

Gabby looked up into his face unable to believe all the changes that had happened in her life. She thought she'd lost everything. Everything she'd never wanted, true, but a life she'd built, and losing it had been hard. Yet, in losing it, she had gained everything she'd always wanted, including some things she hadn't even realized she'd wanted. But she did want them. She really did.

Plumber took a quick phone call. "Yeah. I said yeah, sis. I'll tell her." He stowed his phone.

"Everything okay?" Gabby asked.

"Kelly is expecting us for dinner on Christmas at six.

You're to make brownies. She had one at Alyce's and she wants a double batch for herself, the little glutton. She'll be griping about packing on extra pounds until St. Patrick's Day."

I gave her a tin . . . wait. She wasn't there, so I put them in the back of Sara's van."

Plumber rolled his eyes. "They're gone."

"Sara does love brownies." Gabby laughed hard and deep. *Christmas dinner at six.* This Christmas, she would not be alone . . .

The joy of seeing a promise made to herself fulfilled spread through her.

And just like that, the pain of living a lifetime as blood strangers behind closed doors, keeping the family secrets, was laid to rest.

FAMILYSECRETS.LIFE

WWW.FAMILYSECRETS.LIFE

LOVE TRUMPS BLOOD

They say you can't choose your family.
You just love them anyway.
I guess you can do that, until you can't.
When you're scared out of your wits, alone, and have
nowhere to turn, put out an SOS, then look around and see
who shows up.
Who offers help, refuge, aid? Who doesn't abandon you?
Or hold you hostage for a kindness?
That could be someone related by blood.
But it could also be a friend.
Maybe someone you didn't realize was such a good friend

as he or she proves to be.
Family can be just about anyone.
It isn't blood that makes them so.
It's a spirit of love.

— FAMILYSECRETS.LIFE

SNEAK PEEK

Savage Beauty © 2020 by Peggy Webb

The foundation of every relationship is trust. Whether in friendship or marriage, each partner should be like an inviting and nurturing home with every nook and cranny open to the light of truth. No secrets. No lies.

— FAMILYSECRETS.LIFE

ONE

Ocean Springs could be any other coastal town in the Deep South with its quaint shops and tea rooms overlooking the blue waters of the Mississippi Sound where everything from fishing boats to yachts ride the waves. But the truth of this otherwise sleepy town is far more dramatic.

Ninety miles of barrier islands, lying ten miles offshore, separate the sound from the Gulf of Mexico and create protected waters fed by two great rivers--the Pearl and the Pascagoula. The combination of salt and fresh water forms a sea teeming with plant and animal life.

And many would say secrets.

In the early twentieth century, the wildly eccentric artist Walter Anderson put Ocean Springs on the map by capturing the magic of sea and island on canvas. His art and his history still loom over the town.

But looming even larger is Allistair Manor, a gothic mansion on the highest point in the outskirts of the city that protects the lives, loves and scandals of three generations of Allistairs, the royal family of American horticulture.

Sitting inside her bedroom suite in the second floor west wing of the manor, Lily felt the full weight of the house, the family name, and its legends. This evening she would be introduced to the world as the woman who would soon become an Allistair. This evening her life would change forever.

Her mind told her everything was going to be perfect, but her heart had its own opinion. It beat like the wings of a caged wild bird.

Even the diamond and ruby necklace in the jeweler's box on her dressing table made a statement about her future. Twenty-seven carats of precious stones winked at her with eyes turned fiery in the lamplight, and yet secretive as they nestled among the folds of the black velvet box.

The gift was the latest of many from her fiancé, Stephen, all far too extravagant. Lily was not a diamonds and rubies kind of woman. She wasn't even a lady-of-the-manor kind of girl. She was a practical single mom and interior designer who had moved in with her fiancé a week ago because her lease was about to run out. With the wedding now less than three weeks away, it didn't make sense to pay another year's rent.

Besides, it was far easier to redecorate her new home onsite than to run back and forth from her downtown apartment. And there was the crux of her problem. This was no ordinary house. It was a dark mausoleum filled with outdated furniture and locked rooms.

How could she ever make it a home if there were rooms she couldn't enter? When she'd broached the subject to Stephen, he'd told her the archives of Allistair Roses were housed behind locked doors to protect the horticultural secrets of one of the world's most famous families of rose breeders. Preventing piracy in the business was common.

Still, the very idea of forbidden rooms in her own home had sent her to the new online site, FamilySecrets.life, where a team of psychologists offered advice and private counseling on an array of family issues. She'd been reassured to learn that it was the relationship, not the house, that mattered. She was on solid ground with Stephen.

"I worry too much. That's all."

She could—and *would*--transform the living quarters and turn the house into a home she would love. Hopefully, so would her daughter.

Annabelle was storming down the hallway this very minute, making no bones about her state of mind. Lily would recognize her daughter's combative march anywhere.

"Mom!" Annabelle knocked once but didn't wait for an answer. She swept into the bedroom, her strawberry blond hair in a messy ponytail, her tee shirt untucked from her blue jeans, and her full panoply of teenaged angst on display. "I look dorky in this dress. I don't care if your stupid fiancé did give it to me. I'm not wearing it to the party."

Her daughter tossed the dress onto the bed and crossed her arms over her chest. At fifteen, she was already showing the curves of maturity. Not as much as her best friend Cee Cee, who trailed behind her, but still Lily felt a momentary shock at how quickly time had flown.

It seemed only yesterday Lily had been a teenager herself, fatherless, living on the edge of poverty, and pregnant out of wedlock.

"Let me take a look." When Lily picked up the dress, Annabelle rolled her eyes.

"See! It's *pink*. With *ruffles!*"

Lily wished her fiancé had consulted her first. But when had someone as powerful as an Allistair consulted anybody? Stephen had unilaterally decided to ignore their spring wedding date and book the church for early January. Just thinking about it gave Lily a headache.

Granted, he'd been a bachelor for thirty-nine years. He'd never even come close to marriage, which probably explained why he couldn't come up with a logical reason for the rush. She was definitely going to talk to him. Tonight. After the party.

Now, she said to her daughter, "Stephen meant well." He always did, didn't he?

She really should correct Annabelle about calling him stupid, but she would save that for later. She knew the humiliation of being singled out in front of friends. "He's a good person, and he loves you, Annabelle. You have to *try*."

"I don't care what you say. If I have to wear that dress I'm not going."

An argument over a dress would do nothing but exacerbate the situation.

"Okay. I can accept that."

"Mom, you're the best!" Annabelle gave her a bear hug.

"You're not off the hook. You have to thank Stephen for the dress."An eye roll from her daughter. "And you have to mean it. As soon as he gets back from the airport with his mom, find him and explain that you want to wear the party dress Gran made."

Lily's mom, a seamstress, had died quietly in her sleep at the end of spring. The thought of her mother not getting to see her walk down the aisle with a good man made Lily's heart hurt.

"Okay," Annabelle said. "I can do that." She gave her best friend a high five. "Look at Cee Cee. I don't know why he picked out a little kid's dress for me and gave her one that makes her look like a Hollywood movie star."

Cee Cee was already wearing her gift, a charming blue velvet dress that matched her eyes and set off skin that looked like the finest mahogany. Her curly black hair made a halo around a sculpted face the cameras would love.

"You look beautiful." Lily hugged her close.

From the moment Cee Cee and Annabelle had met in fifth grade, Lily had tucked this shy but endearing child into her heart and under her wing. Cee Cee had never known her father and had been given up by her mother then shuffled from one foster home to another for years. Lily had tried to fill the void. That included inviting her to spend school holidays with them and as much of the summer as her foster parents would allow. To Lily, Cee Cee was part of the family, another child to love.

"When I tried my new dress on, I couldn't take it off," Cee Cee said. "I feel like a princess in a fairy tale. Have you *seen* the decorations downstairs, Lily?"

"Not yet." Lily was as happy as if she'd personally put every decoration in place. Cee Cee deserved a fairy-tale experience, and so much more. She was determined to help this child achieve her dreams.

"There are four gigantic Christmas trees all done in blue and silver," Cee Cee said. "It looks like a castle or something."

Annabelle snorted. "More like the Addams Family. This whole house is creepy. I expect Lurch to pop out from behind one of the stupid locked doors. Every time I go near one I get a lecture about snooping from that old man with the missing pinkie."

Now she'd gone too far.

"You *cannot* talk that way about Stephen's grandfather."

"He does have only nine fingers, which is creepy."

"Annabelle!"

Her daughter raised her hands in mock surrender. "Okay. Sorry, Mom. I'm going out front now to wait for Stephen."

"Be nice to him, and his mother, too," she said, but she wasn't sure Annabelle heard. The girls were already racing off.

Lily slipped out of her robe and into her bath. When Stephen's grandfather Clive escorted her into the party, he'd look every inch the aristocratic patriarch and powerful founder of a Southern family empire. She had no intention of embarrassing the family or herself.

<hr />

Reporters had descended on Allistair Manor from all the major national television and newspaper networks. Some had even flown in from France and Great Britain.

And why shouldn't they? Stephen C. Allistair was unveiling not only his bride-to-be but his latest hybridized creation, a stunning blue rose with white edging. There was nothing like it in Allistair Roses, and very few in the world. Breeders had not achieved a blue rose until eleven years ago, and then their efforts ran more toward lilac than true blue. Stephen's vivid blue rose was so breathtaking it rivaled the

Allistair rose that had started their horticultural empire. His grandfather Clive's world-renowned black rose.

"When is your precious Lily Perkins coming down?" Stephen's mother glided into place beside him at the bottom of the grand staircase. "Reporters from CNN and FOX are already clamoring to interview me."

He tamped down his irritation. "They'll just have to wait, Toni. This evening is not about you."

"Well, it should be."

Of course, that's what she would think. Toni Allistair had always put herself first. She was a super model with bogus claims of Polynesian royalty in her family tree. Additionally, she was considered the reigning matriarch of the Allistair family. A term she hated.

In fact, she hated everything about the family except its founder...and his money. Even if Stephen's father hadn't had health issues, Toni would never have stayed in the marriage. She'd been only too happy to leave her husband in the hands of medical professionals and leave Stephen to be raised by his grandfather.

"If you wanted to be the center of the adoring press, you should have stayed in New York."

"What?" Even when Toni raised her eyebrows, nothing else on her face moved. He'd lost count of the number of face and body lifts she'd had. "And miss meeting my *granddaughter*?" She shivered and cast a disdainful look in Annabelle's direction. "Couldn't you at least have picked a brood mare who didn't have children? Especially a teenager? She makes me look old."

If the press weren't everywhere, Stephen would have walked off. *Brood mare* stung, but Toni wasn't that far off the mark. She never was. That's why she and Clive got along so well. Both were blunt to a fault.

It had been Clive who reminded him of his duty to the family.

You've got to find a wife and have a son to carry on the family tradition, Stephen. I've worked too hard to find the secret to the perfect rose to have it die with the third generation.

Stephen had met Lily this past summer at a benefit to raise money for the Walter Anderson Museum. She was a gorgeous woman with blue eyes and long wavy hair that looked like a sunset, vivid red streaked with gold. All natural. Her daughter was proof she'd bear him a great-looking son, one worthy of the Allistair name.

She was easy-going and easy to love. But the truth was that his work consumed him, especially of late.

That's why he'd moved up the wedding date. The sooner he got Lily pregnant, the quicker he could concentrate on his masterpiece—a rose that would be so impossibly beautiful, he hadn't even confided in his grandfather. His heart sped up just thinking about it.

"Look at what the cats dragged up." Toni nudged him, bringing his attention to the second floor landing where Clive posed with Stephen's fiancée on his arm. Wearing his full silver hair long enough to touch the collar of his tuxedo, he appeared to be a man far younger than eighty-eight. And Lily was simply stunning in the white Christian Siriano gown and heirloom necklace Stephen had given her. "I see the little tramp wasted no time getting her hands on your grandma's diamonds."

Thankfully, the press and the photographers Stephen had hired for the evening were too busy snapping pictures of Clive and Lily to overhear his so-called mother's vicious remarks.

"Toni, retract your claws, or I'll call you a cab to the airport."

"I don't care what you do as long as you don't let that

bedraggled urchin call me grandma." She nodded toward Annabelle then made a beeline for a group of reporters on the other side of the room.

The air seemed fresher without her. At his grandfather's signal, Stephen joined Clive and Lily at the top of the stairs where he announced his engagement with all the fanfare worthy of an Allistair.

With dozens of cameras turned on them, he leaned in and whispered to Lily, "Are you happy, darling?"

"Of course."

Her smile was genuine, and that made everything so much easier for Stephen.

She had to have noticed he didn't introduce Annabelle. But neither had he mentioned his wicked biological gene-pool of a mother. Thankfully, Lily would not be like the narcissistic Toni. And she certainly wouldn't be like his grand-mother, who had been too weak to be an Allistair.

Just as Lily's daughter proved her great genes, her history proved her courage. She'd survived a pregnancy at sixteen, a tumultuous one year marriage to a muscle-bound football player who didn't want her or their daughter, single mother-hood, and the death of both parents. Still, she had managed to earn a college degree in interior design and start her own business.

"Kiss her," someone called.

"I'm happy to oblige." Imagining the picture they made, much like the Duke and Duchess of Cambridge on the balcony of Buckingham Palace, he held the kiss through the frenzy of clapping and congratulations that echoed through the downstairs ballroom. Allistair Roses could only benefit from this kind of publicity.

One of the reporters called, "Roses," and the rest of the crowd took up the chant. "Roses! Roses!"

"Duty calls, Lily. You don't mind finding the girls and

bringing them to the conservatory, do you? Clive and I need to get there ahead of the reporters."

"Of course not. I don't have to be pampered like your greenhouse cultivars."

"You've picked a champion, son, and a stunning one, at that." Clive clapped him on the shoulder then winked at Lily. "I've got to borrow this stud for the Allistair show."

They flanked Lily and escorted her down the stairs then watched until she was out of earshot.

"Don't you think you're laying on the champion brood mare/stud analogy too thick?" Stephen asked.

"I can say a lot of things now that I couldn't when I was your age." Clive, who never displayed remorse about anything, led the way out of the ballroom toward the attached glass conservatory.

Two guards stood on either the door, and four more were strategically placed inside. Stephen nodded at them, but didn't stop to speak. They knew their job. In five minutes they'd remove the gold rope and let the reporters along with Lily and the two girls inside. Afterward, the rest of the guests, which included most of the population of Ocean Springs and the surrounding Gulf coastal area, would be allowed to view the roses in groups of ten.

Colors and fragrances exploded around Stephen. The conservatory was covered with Allistair roses, each with its own pedestal and plaque. In the center stood the black rose. The plaque beneath it said *Clive Allistair, Poe's Raven. "Quoth the raven, Nevermore." Tea rose inspired by Edgar Allan Poe.*

Also showcased in the center was Stephen's latest cultivar. Brilliant blue with white edges. *Stephen C. Allistair* the plaque read. *Mariposa. "Butterflies are white and blue in this field we wander." Floribunda rose inspired by Edna St. Vincent Millay.*

The roses unleashed a thousand memories. Formulas and secrets swirled through his mind. Closed doors and dark rooms whispered while midnight hours and grueling work filled him with both exhaustion and exhilaration. The mystery of the roses filled Stephen until he felt as infinite as the moon casting its silver light through the glass ceiling of the conservatory.

His grandfather's hand on his shoulder brought him back to the moment. "Well done, son."

Together they walked to the small dais at the front of the conservatory and waited for reporters and photographers to gather. All attention and cameras were turned on them until Lily came in with the girls. She and Cee Cee looked stunning, but Annabelle looked flushed and out of sorts.

Clive nodded in her direction. "Is she sick?"

"No. She's stubborn. She hates this house and me, too."

"I suggest boarding school."

"Lily would never stand for it."

Stephen didn't have time to worry about Annabelle, though. Reporters were already firing questions.

"Mr. Allistair, how many cultivars have you originated?"

"Sixty-five," Clive said, and applause thundered through the glass room. "My grandson Stephen has already produced forty-five, and if he lives to be as old as I am, he'll surpass me."

"And what about your son, Wyler?"

It was the question Stephen always dreaded. He was glad to let Clive answer.

"He did only one, but it's spectacular. It buds out deep red, and then the blooms turn to a pale blush. The Vanishing Red is named for the Robert Frost poem by the same name. You'll find Wyler's climber beside the yellow floribunda I created after his mother died."

The reporter from CBS turned to read aloud the plaque on The Vanishing Red. "*It's too long a story to go into now.* Why did Wyler choose such a cryptic quote? Did it have anything to do with him ending up a recluse in Switzerland?"

Clive nodded, handing off the difficult question. Stephen prided himself on being the Allistair family's spin doctor.

"As most of you know, Allistair Roses has many traditions. One of them is naming our roses for literary works or figures. There's no pattern or agenda in the way we select our names. But we do seem to be partial to the poets."

Most of the reporters laughed, but others shouted questions.

"Why has Wyler given no interviews in thirty-eight years?"

"Stephen, how do you respond to rumors that your father is mentally ill?"

"Why does Toni Allistair refuse to talk about her husband in interviews?"

"Why did a beauty like Toni Allistair never divorce Wyler and remarry?"

Making his face a careful mask, Stephen stuffed his hands into his pockets to hide his balled-up fists. He wasn't about to let them keep digging into his family history.

"We have nothing to add to our original statement about my father's rare disease and his subsequent retirement to Switzerland. Thank you for coming. Before you leave, do take the time to say hello to my beautiful fiancée." He gestured to the back of the room where Lily stood with the girls. "Enjoy the food, the music and the roses, especially my new blue and white floribunda, the Mariposa. It was nine years in the making, and we're delighted to add it to the collection of award-winning Allistair roses."

He was turning to leave when a reporter shouted, "What's next for you, Stephen?"

"The Margaret. A blue tea rose so vivid it will be neon." Adrenaline burst through him, and the flush crept over up his neck. "The inspiration is a Carl Sandburg poem by that name." He glanced toward the back of the room. Her face was glowing, and his heart picked up speed as he quoted from the poet. "'In your blue eyes... I saw many wild wishes.'"

The reporters turned their attention and their cameras on Lily, and Stephen rushed from the conservatory. He had to have some air.

We hope you enjoyed this sneak peek of *Savage Beauty*, the next book in the Behind Closed Doors: Family Secrets series.

BEHIND CLOSED DOORS: FAMILY SECRETS SERIES

Don't miss this brand-new series from the bestselling authors of the **STORMWATCH** and **BREAKDOWN** series!

THE LIE Debra Webb
(December 2)
BLOOD STRANGERS Vicki Hinze
(December 9)
SAVAGE BEAUTY Peggy Webb
(December 16)
DEADLY REFLECTIONS Regan Black
(December 23)
FATAL DECEPTIONS Cindy Gerard
(December 30)
Coming in December 2020 in ebook and paperback.

ABOUT THE AUTHOR

VICKI HINZE is the author of nearly forty novels, nonfiction books and hundreds of articles published in more than sixty-three countries. Her books have received many prestigious awards and nominations, including her selection for *Who's Who in the World* (as a writer and educator), nominations for Career Achievement and Reviewer's Choice Awards for Best Series and Suspense Storyteller of the Year, Best Romantic Suspense Storyteller of the Year and Best Romantic Intrigue Novel of the Year. She co-created an innovative, open-ended continuity series of single-title romance novels, an innovative suspense series, and has helped to establish sub-genres in military women's fiction (suspense and intrigue and action and adventure) and in military romantic-thriller novels. Hinze loves genre-blending and blazing new trails for readers and other authors. She is a former columnist for Social-In Global Network and radio host of *Everyday Woman*.

Get Vicki's monthly newsletter at **http://mad.ly/ signups/82943/join**

> **Follow Vicki on Amazon.**
> **Follow Vicki on BookBub.**

Visit her website at www.vickihinze.com

ALSO BY VICKI HINZE

Behind Closed Doors: Family Secrets

Blood Strangers

StormWatch Series

Deep Freeze

Bringing Home Christmas

Clean Read

S.A.S.S. Unit Series

Black Market Body Double | The Sparks Broker | The Mind Thief | Operation Stealing Christmas | S.A.S.S. Confidential

Clean Read

Breakdown Series

so many secrets | her deepest fear (Short Read)

Down and Dead, Inc. Series

Down and Dead in Dixie | Down and Dead in Even |

Down and Dead in Dallas

Clean Read

Shadow Watchers (Crossroads Crisis Center related)

The Marked Star | The Marked Bride | Wed to Death: A Shadow Watchers Short

Clean Reads

Crossroads Crisis Center Series

Forget Me Not | Deadly Ties | Not This Time

Clean Read Inspirational

The Reunion Collection

Her Perfect Life | Mind Reader | Duplicity |

Clean Reads

Lost, Inc.

Survive the Night | Christmas Countdown |

Torn Loyalties

Clean Read Inspirational

War Games Series

Body Double | Double Vision | Double Dare | Smokescreen: Total
Recall | Kill Zone

General Audience (out of print)

The Lady Duo

Lady Liberty | Lady Justice

General Audience

Military

Shades of Gray | Acts of Honor | All Due Respect

General Audience

Paranormal Romantic Suspense

Legend of the Mist | Maybe This Time

General Audience

Seascape Novels

Beyond the Misty Shore | Upon a Mystic Tide |

Beside a Dreamswept Sea

General Audience

Other

Girl Talk: Letters Between Friends I My Imperfect Valentine I
Invitation to a Murder I Bulletproof I The Madonna Key (series co-
creator) I Before the White Rose I Invidia

Multiple-Author Collections

Dangerous Desires I My Evil Valentine I Risky Brides I Smart Women
and Dangerous Men I Christmas Heroes I Love is Murder I Cast of
Characters I A Message from Cupid Seeing Fireworks

Nonfiction Books

In Case of Emergency: What You Need to Know When I Can't Tell
You I One Way to Write a Novel I Writing in the Fast Lane I All
About Writing to Sell I

Mistakes Writers Make and How-To Avoid Them

For a complete listing visit http://vickihinze.com/books

DON'T MISS STORMWATCH

StormWatch Series

Holly, the worst winter storm in eighty years...

Holly blows in with subzero temperatures, ice and snow better measured in feet than in inches, and leaves devastation and destruction in its wake. But, in a storm, the weather isn't the only threat—and those are the stories told in the STORMWATCH series. Track the storm through these six chilling romantic suspense novels:

FROZEN GROUND by Debra Webb, Montana
DEEP FREEZE by Vicki Hinze, Colorado
WIND CHILL by Rita Herron, Nebraska
BLACK ICE by Regan Black, South Dakota
SNOW BRIDES by Peggy Webb, Minnesota
SNOW BLIND by Cindy Gerard, Iowa

Get the Books at Amazon

DON'T MISS BREAKDOWN

The Explosive Suspense Breakdown Series

A ground-breaking, fast paced 4-book suspense series that will keep you turning pages until the end. Reviews describe **BREAKDOWN** as "unique," "brilliant" and "the best series of the year." The complete series includes:

the dead girl by Debra Webb
so many secrets by Vicki Hinze
all the lies by Peggy Webb
what she knew by Regan Black.

You'll want all four books of the thrilling **BREAKDOWN** series!

Get the books at Amazon.